The Tail of the Arabian, Knight

The Tail of the Arabian, Knight

GEOFFREY MARSH

DOUBLEDAY & COMPANY, INC.

GARDEN CITY, NEW YORK

1986

Library of Congress Cataloging-in-Publication Data

Marsh, Geoffrey, 1912–
The tail of the Arabian, knight.

I. Title.
PS3563.A7145T3   1986   813'.54   86–2060
ISBN: 0-385-19101-4
Copyright © 1986 by Doubleday & Co., Inc.
All Rights Reserved
Printed in the United States of America

First Edition

This is for Charles and Kathryn
Who showed me that a man need
never retire.

The Tail of the Arabian, Knight

ONE

The Hillendale Country Morgan Horse Farm never once, in its eighty-three years, raised, sold, or bred a Morgan horse, even in spirit; it was, however, in the country.

More specifically, it was three miles outside the small hillside community of Inverness, in rural northwestern New Jersey, where the land is seldom flat for more than half a mile at a stretch, and the highways, such as they are, are seldom very straight. They generally follow the convoluted contours of the low, wooded hills, and are not much more than blacktopped cowpaths or resurrected coach roads; to ride one at speed is foolhardy at best, stomach-lurching at worst, and to take any one stretch of Jay Hollow Lane at any speed at all will blur the site of Hillendale into invisibility.

The farm itself lies to the right of the lane—forty verdant and rolling acres that begin below the level of the verge, sweep along a flat for two hundred yards, and climb a slope whose crest is thick with a march of white birch, pine, and blue spruce. Brown-and-grey boulders fringed with flowering weeds dot the landscape, a large pond replete with ducks breaks the green, and all of it is fenced in, as much to keep unwanted visitors out as to keep the horses from wandering onto the tarmac.

The 150-year-old farmhouse is two stories high not counting the attic, white clapboard with a peaked roof broken by four chimneys; the windows are high and narrow, and the shutters are green and laddered. The fine condition of the building is evidence of prosperity, but its back is set firmly to the lane to discourage the casual passerby from stopping for a look around.

Hillendale is not known for its hospitality.

And the first visitor in over a month was Lincoln Bartholomew Blackthorne.

It was June at Hillendale, an early afternoon when the jays scolded halfheartedly from their vantage points in the trees, the robins had given up their worm hunt for the day and were searching for suitable dust pools to take a bath in, and the green-capped ducks in the pond were diving for pearls while dragonflies dove for the peaks of their tails. In the various pastures scattered about the farm, horses grazed, or romped, or took care of the game but unsteady foals stumbling along behind. Far beyond the freshly painted red barn a silent tractor sat in the middle of a field of alfalfa, bundles of hay scattered about it, a trio of crows sitting on the steering wheel.

Not a single car had gone by in more than three hours.

None were expected to pass for at least another three.

"Now this," said Macon Crowley with a satisfied sigh, "is the life."

The farmhouse's deep front porch faced the pine-topped hill, and Macon was sitting on the righthand side of a hanging, slatted porch swing facing the front yard—an expanse of vigorous rich green no wider than the house itself and bordered by two rows of fat-boled ancient oaks which transformed the lawn into an Emersonian cathedral's aisle leading to a large white-fenced paddock quite obviously intended for very special use of quite special stock.

"Ah, wilderness! Ah, Rousseau, you old dog! The fresh air, the smell of new-mown hay, the birds singing their lovely hearts out . . ." He shook his head in supreme contentment and brushed a lazy hand down the front of his blue plaid, mother-of-pearl-buttoned cowboy shirt. Around his slightly paunched waist was a silver-and-turquoise concha belt, on his feet a pair of hand-tooled brown boots whose toes came to a rather nasty point, and the jeans he wore were nearly as white as his trimmed white beard. The only thing missing was a ten-gallon hat. "I tell you, it smells exactly like paradise."

"I'll tell you what it smells like," Old Alice said. "It smells like horse." She was sitting with him on the swing, on the edge of the seat so her Greek leather sandals could touch the grey floorboards.

"It's supposed to," he told her tolerantly. "It's a horse farm."

Old Alice adjusted her sombrero with the plastic grapes on the brim and snorted. "Stupid name. A farm is where you plant things, watch them grow, pluck 'em out and eat 'em. I never saw anybody plant a horse except when he was dead. They do not plant horses, do they, Palmer?"

Palmer Crowley lounged in a bentwood rocker on the other side of the steps. His eyes were closed, his double chins gleamed and quivered, his red face shone like a freshly polished ruby. He grunted.

"Told you," said Alice.

"Farren Upshire," declared Macon, "can call it a dairy for all I care. It's still beautiful."

"It still smells like horse."

In the paddock were three energetic and stunning mares—two blacks and a grey. They were not Morgans by any stretch of a blind man's imagination; they were purebred Arabians, and their combined value on a bad day at the market easily exceeded one million dollars.

Macon sighed resignation at Alice's unromantic obstinacy and glanced wistfully over his shoulder. There were three tall windows evenly spaced behind the swing, their white-tufted curtains pulled back, their new white shades raised all the way up. Their screens did not permit a view of the large parlor inside, but he could hear two voices in earnest conversation, low and unintelligible.

"Stop spying," Old Alice said, punching his leg just shy of causing a cramp.

He watched disdainfully as she lit a long violet cigarette with an engraved gold lighter, and blew a series of smokerings that would have gotten her top pay in any European circus. "You fail miserably and without redemption to grasp the romance of the place," he said at last.

"Get stuffed."

"What?"

"Stuffed. Roy Rogers got his horse stuffed, you know. Put him in a museum, I think. Or up in his bedroom. Something like that."

"A splendid animal. Trigger was his name."

"His dog, too."

"A noble beast. Bullet, I believe. A most remarkable German shepherd."

"Probably Dale Evans when she goes."

"The family that stays together—"

She hit him with a grape.

They swung in companionable silence for several minutes while the horses grazed and Palmer snored and the chains that held them up nearly creaked them to sleep.

Finally, Old Alice groaned with not a little boredom and slid off the benchseat, steadied herself, stretched, and walked stiffly to the railing. There she took a deep breath, coughed, lifted the sombrero's floppy brim, and sniffed. "Hey," she said softly, rubbing one hand over her bony hip. A crouch, another sniff. "Hey," she said again.

Macon watched as the grey mare nervously paced the length of the paddock's back fence, tossing her head, snorting now and then before breaking into a short run. Alice crouched lower to see under the eaves to the crest of the hill. Then she sat down, and Macon took her place.

"Better tell Blackie," she said, lighting another cigarette with the butt of the first.

"A squirrel, most likely."

"You ever see a squirrel that looked like Gene Autry?"

"Could be just a rider. There are lots of other farms around here, y'know. He could be just passing by, minding his own business, saw us and wanted to take a picture for his scrapbook."

"Been there a while, right, Palmer? And he doesn't have a stupid camera."

Palmer snored and nodded.

Macon looked around, at the screen door half again as wide as normal. "He doesn't like to be disturbed when he's doing a fitting," he said.

"He measured a circus tent last week. Farren won't know the difference."

Macon hesitated, then strode to the door and knocked on the frame. Waited, and knocked again.

Inside, the voices stopped.

"Well?" said Old Alice as he took his place beside her.

Macon sighed. "Here we go again, I think."

Old Alice grinned. "Good! I hate it when Blackie hasn't got anything to do."

A minute passed, then two, and just as Macon was about to rise and summon Lincoln again, the oversized screen door creaked open, the floorboards shuddered, and Palmer shifted uneasily in his rocking chair.

"What is it, folks?" Farren Upshire asked quietly, squinting at the bright afternoon light. He was just under six feet tall and just over 350 pounds, most of which was gathered solidly around his waist and bulging his trousers to an inordinate degree, thus requiring two stout canes to maintain his balance. His hair was thin and black, his face more folds than creases, and when he spoke so much of him moved that some in his acquaintance have never seen his mouth. He was wearing a pair of trunk-hugging red plaid trousers held up by a pair of red-and-blue suspenders; the waistband almost made it, the rest of the material didn't. His chest was bare, and so thick with black hair that many people believed he always wore a sweater.

Though he was obviously annoyed at being disturbed, the cane in his left hand thumped the floor like a happy dog's tail as he smiled broadly at Old Alice, giving her a wink only a blind woman would take for something amiss with his eye.

Upshire loved only his horses, but lust was a vice he was determined to taste at least once before dying.

"What?" he asked again, face creased into a puzzled frown.

"Need to talk to Blackie," Old Alice said, turning away from his appraisal of her figure with an insulted shrug. Alice had her quirks, but blubber wasn't one of them.

"We're mighty busy in there," he explained in his best love-struck voice. "Lincoln—you know he don't like being tagged Blackie—he ain't quite finished with me yet. Sharkskin's a chore when it comes to a good fit, all them wrinkles and things. A fine tailor that boy is, but he don't know everything yet about sewing and patching. His mind wanders from time to time, if you know what I mean."

Macon wiped a hand over his face.

Alice pulled down the sidebrim of her sombrero.

Upshire ignored what he thought might have been giggles and lumbered to the top step to peer down the stretch of lawn to his favorite horses.

"Lovely," he said with a distinct catch in his voice. "I could just look at them lovely critters for hours. Such lines—so delicate, so perfect. Do you folks know," he said, glancing over his shoulder to be sure they were listening, "that Arabians are the friendliest horses in the world? It's in their nature, that's what it is. Their nature. They'd do anything for their master, long as he treats 'em right." He sighed, and sniffed. "Run their little equine hearts out if they was asked. Yessir. Mighty fine creatures. Mighty fine."

The door opened again, Lincoln stepped out, slender and of medium height, with thick brown hair drooped slightly over his forehead. There was exasperation in his expression, and a cloth ruler draped over one shoulder. He did not squint at the light, and his dark eyes took in Upshire's naked back before turning to Macon.

"What," he said, barely containing his impatience.

"Echo," said Old Alice, and lit another cigarette.

"Company on the hill," Macon told him as he turned to head back inside; the old man jutted his beard like a pointer, moving away from Alice now that Upshire's attention was diverted. "Don't think it's a bird-watcher."

Lincoln stopped.

"Cowboy," said Old Alice.

Lincoln turned.

"On a palomino," said Macon.

"You're kidding."

"White hat, white shirt, white pants, white boots," Alice explained as Lincoln moved behind Palmer and bent down to look up the slope. "If he's dead, he's a damned pretty ghost."

"And I was going to Maine," he muttered in disgust. "My bag is already packed. Tomorrow at dawn I was going to lock up the shop, bury the key, and drive up there for a well-deserved vacation."

"What's in Maine, for god's sake?" Old Alice said.

"Moose. Deer. Raccoons. Lots of tall trees, huge lakes, beautiful streams, and lots of no people to bother me, that's what's in Maine."

"Sounds rather bucolic," Macon said.

"Dull," Alice translated. "With no people you don't have any fun."

"With no people," Lincoln said as he straightened, "I won't get dead, either."

Macon and Old Alice exchanged exasperated glances. Lincoln, when he was feeling like a tailor, was sometimes a glorious pain in the ass. He thought more of himself than he did his friends, robbing them of the excitement they looked forward to now and then. At times they wondered how the man survived.

"The most loyal animals in the world," Upshire crooned, oblivious to the conversation behind him. "That's why I don't have me no dogs on my place. Dogs slobber; horses nuzzle. Dogs gotta be walked; horses crap on their own, no help from nobody. They made me rich, I'll admit it up front, but I'd love them for themselves, even if they hadn't."

Macon nodded as if Upshire could see him, and Palmer raised the pitch of his snoring.

Old Alice was fed up. "The man talks like he was born in a log cabin," she muttered. "Christ, he comes from Jersey City."

"That may as be," Upshire said without looking around, "but a man's birthplace ain't no necessary indication of what he has lodged in his deepest soul."

Macon laughed his approval of the mild scolding, and Alice pelted him with another grape.

Lincoln ignored them all. He moved closer to the railing and scanned the treeline until he saw the man his friends had spotted. Exactly as described, the watcher was directly in line with the porch steps, just to one side of a perfectly formed Scotch pine. His face was in shadow, too distant to discern any features. There was no reason to think he was anything but a casual rider, someone from a neighboring stable on his way to somewhere else and taken by the beauty of the farm's shallow valley.

On the other hand, a casual rider on his way from a neighboring stable to somewhere else did not generally carry a rifle on his saddle.

"Farren," he said, "why don't we go inside and finish up so I can go home?"

Upshire swiveled about ponderously, rebalanced himself on his canes, and shook his massive head. "You just don't give a man a break, do you?"

"Just a few more nips and tucks."

"I ain't seen my horses all damned day!"

"They're not going anywhere."

Palmer stirred, crossed his legs at the ankles, and refolded his hands over his stomach.

"Too hot to stay out here," Old Alice said quickly when Lincoln gave her a commanding look. "Wow, it's murder." She fanned herself with her cigarette.

"Mosquitoes," Macon added, slapping at his neck. "Damned things'll get you every time."

Upshire looked at the pair on the swing, looked at Lincoln and grinned. "You folks, and I know you don't mind me saying this because we're all friends here, but you folks are about the strangest people I have ever met in my life."

"Just looking out for the welfare of a valued client," Lincoln said with a smile, and held out a hand as though to usher the man past him.

Upshire would have answered, but he was interrupted by the loud *crack* of a gunshot, and before anyone could move the huge man toppled slowly to one side.

TWO

Before the sharp sound had faded into the hill beyond the road, Macon was kneeling beside the fat man lying prone on the porch, Old Alice was crouched behind the swing, and Palmer was inside, heading for the sofa.

"Jesus H.!" Upshire exploded as Macon tried to find the wound between rolls and folds of flesh and clothing. "Jesus, the sonofabitch shot my cane!" And he held up the splintered oak staff for Macon to see.

Lincoln had been knocked spinning aside by Palmer's rush for the door, but immediately he recovered, he vaulted the porch railing effortlessly and ran in a half crouch across the lawn toward the Arabians' paddock, keeping the bulk of the trees between him and the hillside. He had no weapons, but he strongly suspected that the assailant, having seen his shot miss and the people scattering on the porch, would not stick around long enough to take another shot.

When the second bullet scattered chips of bark into his face, he dropped to the ground and cursed, crawled to the trunk and looked back to see how the others were faring. Macon was struggling to get Upshire to his feet, Alice beside him with a fresh cigarette in her mouth and her hands angrily on her hips, the brim of her sombrero flapping like wings as she muttered something to the old man and jabbed an accusing finger in the air. Ahead, the Arabians, startled by the gunfire, were thundering around the paddock, tails high and eyes showing white.

A minute passed, another, and he rushed for the last tree. A swift search from each side, and the man in white was gone, the back of his palomino just vanishing into the shadows of the pines.

He could, he knew then, safely return to the farmhouse, but he also knew that having tried once and failed, the man could very easily set himself up along the roadside to try again when Lincoln and the others headed for home. And there was no time to ponder the logic of it, or the possibilities.

He broke from his cover then and clambered over the fence, wasted no time cornering the grey and leaping onto her back. Astonished, she reared once, bucked once, twisted her neck in an attempt to bite his foot, but his hands were firmly buried in her mane and his legs were just as firmly clamped around her sides. With a whisper her ears pricked up, with an urging she galloped for the back, and just as he thought she'd decided to plow directly through the fence and save them both some time, she gathered her strength and leapt. Flew. Landed nimbly on the other side without missing a step and plunged up the hill.

Most of the trees had been cleared to a point just past midway, and he hunched his shoulders, clenched his teeth in gun-shy anticipation until they were well inside the protection of the forest. Once there it was a matter of picking the quickest path through the underbrush until they reached the crest. A brief word slowed the mare, another stopped her, and he scanned the woodland twilight carefully.

There was no noise beyond the chattering birds startled into movement.

He could see no flash of white on any side, and finally urged the grey forward. They rode along the top, pine boughs sweeping down toward his head, dead branches aiming for his sides and chest. The needles on the ground muffled their passing, and it wasn't long before he felt confident enough to cluck the horse into a canter, pressure her into a gallop that finally brought them out of the trees.

A wide meadow lay below, woods on three sides, and the man in white had just reached the midpoint.

Lincoln stared, then leaped forward and whispered, "Fetch."

The grey bolted down the slope, nearly throwing him from his precarious seat, and the sound of her hooves turned the White Rider around. He gaped, shook his head in angry disbelief, and whirled his mount around to charge off to the left. Lincoln angled toward him, trying to breathe in the wind blasting past his face, trying to keep his thighs from cramping.

One hundred yards separated them by the time he reached the bottom of the slope.

Fifty yards when the White Rider reached the trees and yanked his rifle from its saddle sheath.

Thirty by the time he was able to twist awkwardly around and bring the weapon to his shoulder.

Ten by the time he could aim and pull the trigger for the first time.

Lincoln veered sharply to the right with a frantic press of his knee, and the palomino shied at the firing, just enough to throw the gunman off balance, just enough for Lincoln to draw alongside him and leap from the mare's back before he could pull the trigger again.

The man grunted as Lincoln's arms encircled his chest, his shoulder plowing smartly into his side. They swayed for a moment, then toppled to the ground, air forced from their lungs, elbows and legs stinging. Linc rolled over, groaning, and struggled to his knees. The White Rider, however, was already up, and when Linc rubbed a stiff hand over his eyes to clear his vision, the man began to smile.

He was no taller than the tailor, but his chest was more narrow, his arms more sticks than muscle, and he had the narrowest waist Lincoln had ever seen on a man.

But it was the face glaring down at him that stopped him from lunging forward in an attempt to trip him, a face he was positive he had seen more than once in his nightmares. He blinked and stared, knowing he should move yet unable to do so—the face was sallow, long and thin, the chin coming amazingly to an absolute point; the eyes were set so deeply it was impossible to tell their color; and the ragged wisps of hair that straggled from beneath his Stetson were a dead, flat white.

Until his own eyes focused, Lincoln thought a skull was grinning down at him.

Then, without warning, the White Rider laughed bitterly and lashed out with a sharp-pointed boot.

It was easy to escape the arc of the first blow, less easy to escape the second, which caught him high on the shoulder and drove him backward.

A third kick was trapped when he caught the boot by its heel and yanked it toward him. It should have thrown the man to the ground; what it did was take the boot off and leave Lincoln sitting there openmouthed while the man threw the rifle at his head and jumped back into the saddle.

The palomino reared, and Linc threw up his hands.

The grey whickered and charged, and the White Rider sawed frantically on the reins, drove his spurs into his mount's sides, and vanished into the trees.

Slowly, feeling every bruise erupting along his limbs and burrowing into his marrow, Lincoln staggered slowly to his feet and brushed off his clothes. The mare stood patiently beside him, grazing until he patted her neck and she braced herself for the clumsy climb onto her back.

Twenty minutes later he was back on the porch, staring down at the wreckage of the swing. The bolts had been pulled from the ceiling, and the seat was split as if taken to by an ax. Macon came out just as he reached the door.

"What the hell happened here?"

Macon scratched his beard thoughtfully and sniffed. "I misjudged, I believe. I thought he had that darn thing fixed to hold his weight."

Lincoln said nothing. He brushed by the old man and stalked into the parlor where Alice was sitting in an armchair, nibbling on a sandwich, Palmer was asleep and murmuring on the loveseat, and Upshire was on the sofa, mopping his face with an already soaked handkerchief.

Lincoln threw the boot into the man's lap.

Alice grinned.

Palmer snored.

Upshire pushed the boot aside distastefully and waved Lincoln to a seat.

The invitation was refused. Instead, he pushed aside the coffee table and stood in front of Upshire, hands fisted in his pockets, a scowl on his face.

"Farren," he said, "don't you dare if you love living tell me you don't know anything about that."

"Lincoln!" the fat man said, shocked and insulted, his hands spread wide. "Linc, how can you say that a poor farm boy from New Jersey knows anything about a trigger-happy cowpoke from the wilds of the Southwest."

Alice burped.

"Oh my," said Macon from the doorway.

"And how," Lincoln asked, instantly hating himself for asking, "did you know he was from the Southwest?"

"Once upon a time," Upshire began when Lincoln demanded to know what was going on, "and you gotta let me say this in my own humble way or it ain't gonna be said, you understand?"

"If you get on with it, yes," Lincoln told him, his eyes less than slits, his mouth hard, his voice harder still. "Just get on with it, Farren, and don't make me mad."

Upshire found no help in a silent appeal to Old Alice and Macon, and licked his thick lips apprehensively several times before clearing his throat and nodding. "You gotta understand the problem here, Linc."

Lincoln hesitated for a moment, trying to decide whether to strangle him or walk out; then he knelt in front of him and took hold of his wrists, turning them inward until the man's eyes started to water. "I understand that I was nearly killed out there, my friend, and I don't much care for it. Now if you're going to stall, I'm going to leave. If you're going to tell me, then tell me."

Upshire gasped when his wrists were released, and took several deep breaths while he gingerly rubbed the circulation back. "Just . . . just hear me out, son, all right?"

"I'm listening, Farren."

He put his hands to his face as if praying for strength, then stared at the ceiling and started again.

"Lincoln, my doctor has told me that I am going to die by the end of the year lessen I get myself shed of this weight I carry around me."

"Oh."

"And it is clear, too clear, that a mere diet of berries and bark ain't gonna do it."

"Oh."

"Which is why I found myself . . . well, you might call it a kind of almost practically miraculous solution."

"Oh . . . damn."

"Y'see, once upon a time, and it must have been many, many centuries ago, though I'm not all that sure of my dates, there appeared in that mystical far-off land of ancient Arabia a breed of horse completely unlike any ever known by mankind to date. Proud, loyal, sleek, and swift. Stunningly elegant, unmatched anywhere for equine beauty and grace. The sheiks prized them higher than any of their wives and went to war for them at the drop of a sheet; foreigners demanded them and were told to take a hike; the unwashed plebeians of the desert set believed them to be veritable gifts from the gods and in many places worshiped the hell out of them. You would not believe, Lincoln boy, the cults which grew up around them, the magic attributed to them, the fanaticism which surrounded them in the early days before civilization discovered oil under the sand and they were traded in for Mercedeses. It was, to put it mildly, incredible."

"I imagine so," Linc said warily. "And it'll be just as incredible if this fairy tale has anything to do with my nearly getting killed."

"It does, m'boy, it does."

"That," he said, "is what I'm afraid of."

Alice choked on an olive, and Palmer stirred.

"Naturally enough," Upshire continued, his face still wet with perspiration, his eyes avoiding the harsh, daring glare Lincoln gave, "legends grew up around them."

"Naturally."

"A few are damned amusing."

"I am not amused."

"Right." Upshire squirmed, and reached out to touch the white boot gingerly. "Y'see, one of the most fascinating of these here little campfire stories deals with a huge critter that belonged to some desert honcho what called himself Abalar-Ul-Bar-Abadar. Not a nice feller, as I understand it. Magician, wizard, or something like that."

Lord, Linc thought, but no one moved to save him.

"Big black thing—the horse, that is—and mean as horseshit in August. Don't know what the guy looked like, probably wore a sheet and stuff like them Arab folks do. Anyway, he rode that critter around for years, raping and pillaging and casting his spells and generally making a fine mess of things out there in the dunes, until someone managed to bag him. Don't know who, and it don't matter none, but when the battle was over, the horse was the only thing left of Abadar and his reign. That's right, Linc, nothing left but that damned horse.

"Ain't no one wanted it, though. Nobody could ride it, see, seeing as how it belonged to Abadar there, and I told you them Arabians are damn loyal animals. Finally, so the story goes, the kid that killed the magician cut off the critter's mane and tail to make it impotent, so to speak, and that's the end of that."

"No, it isn't," Lincoln said.

"You're right, boy! God, are you astute."

"I am impatient, Farren. Very impatient. I ask you politely before I ask not so politely—so what?"

"The tail, Lincoln. It has . . ." Upshire seemed embarrassed, but his eyes glittered with what Lincoln saw, astonished, were tears. "The tail has qualities, Lincoln. It was braided and twined through with gold thread and some baubles, and it has . . . curative powers." He looked up then, and Lincoln saw him as never before—a man given the death penalty and no way around it unless he believed in something that no one else did. "Lincoln, I am going to die by Christmas and there's no getting around it. I know I'm being drastic, maybe even stupid, but goddamnit, I don't want to die."

"No one does," Lincoln had said softly.

"Yeah. I suppose. But that cowboy out there, the one who tried to shoot me? He wants what I want—and he knows that I know where to get that tail."

Well, great, Lincoln had thought. Farren's after a pipe dream, and some damned fool cowboy already thinks I'm on the case. It had to be that because he knew that Upshire had no enemies other than those he'd acquired in his trade; he, on the other hand, had more enemies who wanted to see him retired than any tailor in the universe. It came with the territory. And it wasn't a lot of fun.

"If he knows," he'd said then, "why don't you tell him?"

"Because if I do, he'll kill me."

"If you don't, he'll kill you anyway."

Upshire managed the first smile in an hour. "Nope. Because if he kills me, he's never gonna know."

Linc thought for a moment, not at all liking where his mind was going. "Then if you tell me—"

"Right," Upshire said.

It was then that Lincoln groaned and walked out of the house.

THREE

Inverness was spread across a low and wide hill, the houses old and well kept, the town square a brilliant and cool green, its wood-and-iron benches filled now with people watching the traffic thin, the birds finding their roosts, the pedestrians slowing, and the sky turning a soft indigo. No one looked at the '36 lemon yellow Cord convertible that poked its way around the square. Everyone knew Alice, and since she wasn't leaving town, there wasn't anything to see.

Alice, ignoring the municipal government's provided amenity of curbing, parked half on the sidewalk on Creek Road, Inverness's three-block main street off the square. Between a garishly red-signed drugstore and Ginny's Olde Time Tavern was a tiny shop with narrow display windows flanking a recessed doorway. In the window was a female mannequin wearing a lovely prom gown that showed more cleavage than most teenagers would have in their lives; on the windows it said simply, "Tailor."

In front was a long green wooden bench shaded by a maple that reached the second, topmost floor of the building. Macon, Old Alice, and Palmer leapt from the car and took their places on the bench before Lincoln could move. They would wait, he knew, until Ginny's Happy Hour began, and then move on.

A two-fingered salute from Macon as he passed, fumbling in his pockets for his keys.

"What are you going to do, Blackie?" asked Old Alice as she lit a cigarette.

"Go to Maine," he told her sourly.

"Good for you! The man's a loon."

"He's not a loon," Macon chided. "He's scared to death of his heart bursting."

"Then he should eat tacos and lettuce instead of all that crap he hides in his kitchen. He's got a big enough larder in there to feed the Russian Army. Seems to me, if you're asking, that niece of his should take better care of him."

"I wasn't asking, but he is, may I remind you, a grown man. He can take care of himself."

"Like you, right?" She puffed on the cigarette and blew five perfect smokerings, one inside the other.

Lincoln allowed himself a smile. Despite Upshire's fantastic story, and his equally fantastic request, life went on, nothing changed, and maybe he really and honestly was going to get to go to Maine.

He found the key he needed and hefted it in his palm, but something made him pause before going in. Something missing in the way he arrived home.

A thoughtful glance over his shoulder. Directly opposite was the Inverness Tape and Record Shoppe, owned by the proud and vociferous Estanza family from Inverness by way of Seville, whose eldest daughter, Carmel, was a devoted schoolteacher determined in the face of all odds to put Lincoln's bachelorhood to a merciful, and self-serving, end. Macon approved; Alice did not—she thought Carmel too brazen, too outspoken, too damned modern, chasing men as if she had no pride in herself. Macon thought that was bunk; Alice did too, but she felt that her age compelled her to be old-fashioned on occasion.

Lincoln sided with both, and silently wished Carmel had just a little more self-control when she was out on safari. In fact, he half expected her to race out the Shoppe door the moment he showed himself, and was somewhat disappointed when she didn't. Carmel, for all the uncomfortable feelings she caused in him, was a delight, and if it weren't for the fact that she had ambitions for him he didn't want, didn't need, and didn't aspire to himself, he might have seriously considered giving in to her just to see what it would be like.

It sure as hell wouldn't be dull.

The key warmed in his hand, and a sudden breeze that set the maple to whispering reminded him that if he wanted to leave on his vacation before midnight, he'd best get himself started before he got himself trapped. Afterward, when he returned, he would consider going after Upshire's delusion.

The key went into the lock.

Poor Farren, he thought. Lord, how desperate can you get?

The bolt turned.

Lord, Maine is going to be great this time of year.

And he had taken one step inside when the bomb exploded.

The force of the explosion behind him shoved him viciously over the threshold, but not off his feet. Immediately, with an oath muffled by the echoes of the blast, and his ears ringing louder than Notre Dame in its heyday, he spun around and raced back outside. Macon was standing dumbfounded at the curb, a protective arm tightly around a trembling Old Alice; Palmer was nowhere to be seen.

Across Creek Road the plate glass window of the Tape and Record Shoppe was shattered into glittering triangles on the pavement, and thick curling smoke billowed from the inside. Linc sprinted over, heedless of the snarled and gawking traffic, hearing faintly the high wail of the firehouse siren. He called out as he ran, looking hopefully at the Estanzas' apartment windows over the store for some sign of life. But the curtains remained unruffled, the shades were still drawn, and without a second thought he threw an arm up to protect his face and plunged through the open doorway.

Plastic from the displays in the window and along the walls popped and crackled like fire as he made his way as quickly as he dared through the wreckage, stumbling over toppled racks and scattered discs, swinging his free arm back and forth while he hunted for victims and wondered why there were no flames. But the heat was less intense than he'd been prepared for, and the heavy smoke coursed swiftly out to the street. Within moments after his arrival the store was virtually clear, and he could see that whatever device had been used had not been meant to destroy, but to warn. He had seen it before—noise, smoke, a little flame perhaps, chaos definitely, and definitely not a gas main backfire or a careless cigarette.

Anxiously, he checked the narrow space behind the counter before his lungs protested the acrid sting and the stench of melting plastic was too great to bear. Stumbling this time from lack of oxygen, he returned to the sidewalk, fell to his knees gagging and coughing just as the first fire truck pulled up and someone grabbed him under the arms.

It was Macon, who virtually carried him back to the bench where Old Alice spent an incredibly long time thumping his back to clear his lungs. He spat black phlegm into the gutter. His eyes felt filled with sand. He accepted a damp cloth and wiped his face and the back of his neck, and stared in bewilderment as Creek Road gradually filled with spectators while the volunteer firemen made a grand show of saving the shop.

No one spoke to him.

No one, after he'd been pulled away, even looked in his direction.

"Hell of a job," Macon said.

"Clumsy," said Alice, taking out a cigarette, looking to the fire trucks, and putting it back. "Full of sound and whatever the hell, and it don't mean a damned thing."

"I don't get it," Linc said at last. "What could Carmel have done to deserve that?"

Suddenly, over the chattering noise of the crowd and the blast of the fire hoses, he heard a high-pitched shriek. A woman's high-pitched shriek. The shriek of a woman not done in by grief but galvanized by rage.

Macon cleared his throat, and Old Alice moved down to the other end of the bench.

Lincoln could see bystanders being shoved to one side, could follow by the curses and glares the progress of the enraged woman as she made her way toward the shop, had a few words with the fire chief, then pushed her way directly to him.

She was dark-haired and slender, faintly olive-skinned, and wearing a pair of black jeans too snug for a man's emotional comfort. Her black eyes were fuming, and her hands were fisted tightly against her hips.

"Lincoln, what the *hell* is going on here?"

"Someone tried to blow up your store, I guess," he said, reaching out to pull her down beside him.

She shook her head slowly and leaned against him for a moment.

"My father's gonna kill me. He takes the whole family back to Seville, I'm in charge of the whole capitalist enchilada, and this has to—'*someone*'?" She gaped. "What do you mean, 'someone'? That fireman said it was a spark from a gas line they're fixing up the street."

"Yeah, that could be," he admitted with a straight face. "I guess I was just . . . that is, I thought . . . well, this is hardly New York, I suppose."

"Damn right," she muttered, anger settling to a simmering liberally laced with despair. "God, he's going to kill me and farm me out to a convent."

"He'll understand."

"Oh sure. All he understands is that you must wear garters and girdles at night because you won't marry me and get me out of the classroom. Jesus, will you look at that!" She was on her feet again before he could stop her, shoving and running back to the store to prevent the volunteer firemen from pumping water through the upstairs windows, trying at the top of her well-trained voice to explain that what they wanted was downstairs and didn't they know what a mess they were making?

He watched for another ten minutes before rising. Then, without saying a word, he went into the shop. The display cases on either side of the central aisle reflected the whirling red lights from outside, turning the wares colors he didn't want to see. Coughing still, and thumping his chest with a fist, he made his way through a beaded curtain at the back into a small room where he collapsed into an age-beaten armchair. The floor was barely covered by a haphazard series of worn throw rugs, there was a refrigerator on the lefthand wall, faded prints elsewhere, and a table from the Thrift Shop in the center. On the righthand wall was a full-length poster of Clint Eastwood in his serape, slouch hat, and full armory.

He coughed again and wiped his mouth with a sleeve, leaned his head back and closed his eyes.

The crowd noise subsided.

Within an hour he heard the fire engines start up, stall, start up again, and leave.

Twenty minutes after that the street was quiet.

The beads rattled then, but he didn't move.

"A mess," Macon offered.

He nodded.

"Wasn't meant for her, though. Think somebody probably got the wrong address."

"Yeah. I was thinking the same thing," he said, barely moving his lips. The presence of Eastwood did that to him.

"Cowboys don't use bombs."

"I was thinking that, too."

"Okay. Just didn't want you to think Roy Rogers was a terrorist."

"Never crossed my mind, Macon."

"Tim McCoy, maybe, but not Roy Rogers."

He smiled just enough to send Crowley away, and waited until he heard the beads rattling again. One of these days he was going to get himself a real curtain; maybe even a real door.

"Did you ever think," said Old Alice, "that the old fart has an autographed picture of Lash LaRue in his living room?"

"Never."

"Well, he does. Black-and-white glossy, in a silver frame. I think he wants to put candles in front of it, but he's afraid the Pope might drop in."

Lincoln shifted his legs to cross them, ankle over ankle.

"Had a quick one at Ginny's."

"A little early, isn't it?"

"She says she isn't one to be nosing around the street like some people I could mention, the old fart, but she happened to be at the window a while ago."

He waited.

"Seems like there was a couple of guys there, went into the shop and came right out. Didn't have any packages, didn't buy any records. Just went in and came out."

He grunted; he was listening.

"They were cowboys."

"Great."

"Boots, hats, the whole works."

"Wonderful."

"She didn't think anything of it because of all the farms and stuff around here, but she thought she oughta mention it."

"Good for her."

"I told her it wasn't worth remembering anymore. Customers come and go all day in a place like that, browsing, not buying, lousing up the economy."

"Good for you."

"One of them was all in white."

"Hell."

"The other one was in black."

"You're kidding."

The beads rattled for an answer and he waited again, until Carmel came through, shoving the curtain aside and banging the beads so hard against the wall that he winced. A loud sigh to let him know she was there, and she perched on the edge of the table; he only opened his eyes when it groaned.

"This wouldn't happen if you'd listen to my father," she said, smiling, though he could see the tears bunched in her eyes. "I wouldn't have to play teacher *and* part-time shopkeeper if I could play housewife."

"Life," he said, "is not run on a lesson plan."

She laughed and covered her face with her hands. He let her cry, did not go to her, and when she was done, she stood directly in front of him. "I've got work to do. Pop gets back tomorrow with the troops and he'll have a cow if he sees the store the way it is." A pause. "You want to help?"

He smiled. "I'll be over in a few minutes."

"We could take off our clothes, you know." She grinned. "They wouldn't get dirty that way."

"That's true."

"Then you'd have to marry me because everyone in town would see us and we'd be compromised."

He began to squirm. "Carmel, listen—"

"Or we could just wear our underwear. I have a red bra on." She winked. "Sort of. Actually, it's sunburn, but we could tell them it's a bra."

"Carmel—"

She cocked a hip at him, winked again, and headed for the doorway. On the way, she brushed a finger over his ear. "I think red is a great color."

"So did Hester Prynne."

"Yeah, but she wore it on the outside. Very tacky."

The beads clattered, and he released the breath he'd been holding. Carmel, at times, could be very trying. But there was admiration, too, for the way she was holding up. Right now she had a mammoth job ahead of her, a mystery that would never be resolved as far as she was concerned, and her Spanish family was on its way back to a disaster. She'd be lucky to last the weekend once her father got hold of her; and he'd be lucky to last the night if she knew what he was planning.

Slowly, he rose, then, and walked to the poster, punched the shells on Eastwood's bandolier in a programmed sequence, and stood to one side to allow the hidden door to swing open. It did, knocking him flat against the wall just as he remembered that Palmer had rehinged it. His skull cracked against plaster, the air left his lungs in a hurry, and it was several seconds before he was able to climb the narrow staircase to the apartment above.

The front room was unimpressive, furniture gathered without regard to style or color coordination. If he liked sitting in it or looking at it, he bought it; if it didn't take up too much room and had flat surfaces to pile things on, he bought it; and if its appearance served to conceal the money he'd salted away in a few banks, a few hiding places, and a few accounts not known to the rapacious IRS, he bought it.

The sofa, thickly upholstered and genially lumpy, took him with a creak of pleasure, and the telephone on the cobbler's-bench coffee table rang the moment he put up his feet. He stared at it, thinking it was either Carmel trying to lure him out, or Farren trying to lure him into doing something completely stupid. It wasn't that he minded helping a friend, and he did not begrudge the occasional spate of excitement. But he drew the line at quixotic adventure.

On the other hand, someone had tried to kill him.

On the third hand, someone had tried to blow Carmel up.

The telephone kept ringing and he snatched at the handset, frowning as he thought of what he would say.

"Blackthorne?"

It wasn't Carmel.

"Blackthorne, it was no mistake."

And it wasn't Farren Upshire.

"I just want you to know that I'm going to kill you."

And before Lincoln could answer, the dial tone buzzed.

FOUR

"Nuts," Lincoln said. "Son of a . . . nuts."

He stared at the mute handset for almost a full minute, then replaced it with a slam into its cradle, jumped when the bell rang at the collision, and nearly picked it up again.

"Now who the hell does he think . . . who the hell . . . ?" He put his palms to his temples to stop his brain from running wild, then lowered his hands and told himself it was not going to do him any good if he got himself riled and couldn't think straight.

A few breathing exercises, then, to calm his slowly shredding temper. A few shadow punches at the wall to snap the tension from his limbs. Another deep breath, a long exhalation, and several swift swallows to purge his throat of acid bile. Then he went to the window and saw Carmel alone in the doorway of her shop. She had a broom in one hand, a mop in the other, and her blouse was streaked with mud mixed with ashes. If she got any angrier, he thought sympathetically, she'd explode where she stood. When she turned her head, he moved back so she couldn't see him, and shook his head in disgust at the lengths some people would go to just to get him to work.

I'm going to kill you, the caller had said.

At least, Lincoln thought, he knew where he stood.

"Y'know," he said to the room, "this isn't a bit fair, damnit, and I'm not having a good time."

I'm going to kill you.

"The hell you are," he muttered, and he kicked at the cobbler's bench, kicked at the armchair, then glared at the window and almost threw the telephone through it.

Nuts; and all he had wanted to do was finish Upshire's suit and get away for a while—to unwind, commune with nature, talk to a moose to see how things were going in the wild. Was that too much to ask? Isn't a simple, small-town tailor entitled to a vacation now and then? Damn, did they think he was a doctor or something, on call twenty-four hours a day, bags packed, ready to roll at the first crinkle of money, the first scent of danger, the first twitch of excitement?

But after all this time, he should have known better.

Plans made were plans unmade, as his mother used to say to his father without explaining herself, and the next time he decided to get away from it all, put up his feet and enjoy the quiet, he was just going to go and not tell anyone. That way they would have to solve their own problems and leave him in peace.

A voice; Carmel talking earnestly, and not very quietly, to someone on the street.

His eyes narrowed slightly. Aside from—though not too far aside from—the danger to himself, he definitely did not appreciate the near destruction of her store, nor the implication that none of his friends were immune from attack. That sort of play was a flagrant violation of the rules he had established when he started this fool game. Out in the field, as it were, all bets were off when it came to survival; here in Inverness, however, there was protocol to be observed, and whoever planted the bomb was deliberately flaunting him.

And the telephone call. That was also against those very same rules.

It wasn't so much the call itself and its warning that tended to annoy him—he'd had plenty of those before. But it was the fact that someone he did not know, some total murderous stranger, knew where he lived, and that same total and murderous stranger he did not know also had access to his phone number—knowing full well that he would be the one to answer and not Brother Timothy, the world-traveling, independently wealthy friar whose name was on the lease and who supposedly occupied these rooms whenever he was in town.

There were, as a matter of fact, only four people who knew the truth—his friend George Vilcroft was one, Macon and his cronies the others.

Until now.

He groaned, boxed his ear once for even thinking he might be able to get out of this one, and flopped wearily onto the sofa. Another groan just to be sure that Someone in Charge knew how put-upon he was, and he decided that he might as well get on with it before anything else happened. He grabbed up the telephone and after a moment's thought dialed a local number, and within seconds he was arguing heatedly, then shrugging resignedly and nodding as if the speaker could hear him. When the call was finished, and he had finished cursing Farren Upshire for the disruption of his simple life, he dialed three more numbers in swift succession and gave terse orders not questioned once.

Ten minutes later, after watching the Shoppe for a while and seeing that Carmel's friends had gathered around to help her, he was fumbling around in the kitchen, making a quick dinner before leaving. A single stunted candle flickered on the sink in the window-less room, and he scorched his fingers twice testing the progress of the hash he was frying in the skillet. Each time he did, he swore loudly, vehemently, wishing to hell people would leave him alone just once. He had never been to Maine. He wanted very badly to go to Maine. He wanted to see a moose. The way things were going, the only moose he ever would see would be in the Labor Day parade, strutting potbellied next to an Elk and just behind an Eagle, or a Beaver, or whatever the hell.

He ate standing up at the stove.

He used too much catsup.

He burned his tongue.

There was no milk left, so he had to drink water.

He was in no mood for jokes, then, when someone downstairs punched Clint Eastwood and swore loudly when the door struck an unsuspecting chin, and he was forced to pull down the shade, close the tattered curtains, and switch on the lamp.

It was Macon.

He sat on the sofa and looked at the assortment of papers and folders the old man had spread on the cobbler's bench from his place in the armchair.

"Eastwood nearly took out my dentures," Macon said, rubbing his jaw.

"I'll get it fixed."

"It hits Alice, she'll go right through the wall."

"I said I'd get it fixed. What do you have for me?"

Macon tossed a thick manila folder into his lap, leaned back, and folded his hands contentedly across his stomach. A burp made him blush. Lincoln waited. Macon sniffed.

"You're Stanley Ripshaw, a small-time arms dealer from Liverpool. Passport is stamped with twelve different countries, visa is good; I could only get five letters of introduction done in the time allotted because I can't do miracles when I'm dressing to take the old fart to the movies."

"Macon—"

"I think, however, it's a good cover. Gets you into the underworld with a minimum of fuss."

"Look, Macon—"

"It's chancy, I know, but you've pulled off worse in your time, as I recall."

"Macon, for heaven's sake, what the hell would an arms dealer be doing in New Mexico?"

Macon blinked. *"New* Mexico?"

"Yes."

"I thought you said Mexico."

"I can see that," he said, closing the folder with a sigh.

"Why New Mexico?"

"Because that's where Farren says I can find the tail."

"You've always got Carmel, you know."

"Macon."

Macon looked woefully at the carefully prepared identification he had created. "Maybe you're a renegade wetback bounty hunter or something."

"Macon."

Macon combed a hand through his beard and shook his head. "Do they use pesos out there?"

"Not hardly."

"Then Alice is going to have a fit."

"*New* Mexico?"

"Yes."

Alice looked mournfully at the thick envelope on the cobbler's bench. The plastic grapes wobbled. "First I get clobbered by a pulped cowboy, then this. Hell, what a miserable, rotten day." She lifted a penciled blue eyebrow. "You sure?"

"I'm sure."

"That's what Farren said?"

"Yes."

"You believe a man that looks like a giant pear?"

"Alice—"

"New Mexico. Boy. I didn't even know it had become a state. Does Arizona know that? Boy, I'll bet—oh hell." She rubbed at her nose, and sighed, very loudly. "New Mexico, for god's sake."

Lincoln snapped his fingers to regain her attention. "The legendary horse was supposed to have been brought out there once it was defused, as it were. Somehow Spain got itself a few Arabians, this one in the bunch, and decided to take them on a trip. The Spaniards were very big on exploring deserts, I think."

"What's its name?"

"Knight."

"As in after sunset?"

"As in Ivanhoe."

"For god's sake, what the hell kind of name is that for an Arabian horse?"

"What the hell am I doing chasing after its stupid tail?"

Alice shrugged; Lincoln had been in more preposterous situations. Then she looked at the envelope in her hand. "What am I going to do with all these pesos?"

He sighed. "Alice, the banks are closed. I need money, and this isn't going to do it."

She scratched under her chin, flopping the sombrero's brim against her nose as she reached into her handbag. From her wallet she pulled a vast roll of money from which she peeled off a dozen or so bills.

"My life savings."

"I appreciate it."

"Interest rates are going back up."

"If I get back, I'll pay it."

"What about a few pesos for the natives?"

"The natives are Indians. They don't use pesos."

"Wampum?"

"Alice—"

"Get Palmer to fix that door again, or next time I'll be wearing a catcher's mask."

Palmer lowered his bulk with an expressive silent moan into the armchair and reached into his checkered suit's pockets. A gun, a knife with a wrist spring-sheath, a blackjack, and a small leather case appeared on the bench.

"Tools of the trade, Blackie," he said with a smile. Then he grimaced at Lincoln's look. "Sorry. I forgot."

Lincoln, without saying a word but wishing they'd stop using that nickname when he was around because it made him sound like someone in a trenchcoat, scooped up the revolver and slipped it into his pocket, strapped the sheath and knife on his right wrist, and set the blackjack in his hip pocket. Then he pulled the case to him, opened it, and saw inside a syringe and a green vial nestled in grooved black velvet. A puzzled look, and he picked up the vial, peered at the clear liquid inside and was about to shake it when Palmer hissed at him in a panic.

"What?" he said, replacing the vial quickly, pulling his hands back as if they'd been burned.

"Shake it too much and it'll blow up."

He blinked. "Nitro?

"Sort of. A special compound of my own. Something I do on the weekends."

"Then why the needle?"

"It's also a soporific. Like Alice, it puts you to sleep for twenty-four hours."

"And if I shake the guy who gets it?"

"Nothing. It only works that way when it's in the bottle."

"Beautiful."

Palmer rose and headed for the stairs. "I hinged Clint wrong, I see."

"Yeah, I know."

"Be careful."

"Thanks, I will."

"A good thing I have great reflexes. Man my age can't be dodging doors like that."

He stood to one side of the window and watched the street fade the rest of the way into night. Traffic was gone, the shop windows dark, the only sign of life a bulb burning in the Tape and Record Shoppe as Carmel continued to clean up from the explosion. A few more neighbors had joined her, and from the sound of it an impromptu block party was in progress. Even Ginny had rolled over a barrel of her secret beer. He sighed wistfully, and was about to fetch his bags when he heard a peculiar sound on the blacktop. At first he didn't recognize it, not until he set his palms on the sill and leaned out.

To his right, down by the square, he saw someone coming toward him.

Fast.

On one of the largest horses he had ever seen in his life.

He gaped when the animal trotted down the white line, gaped when it was reined to a thundering halt in front of his door, and gaped again when he saw the rider in the silver-trimmed black saddle.

It was a woman, and as she slipped off the beast's back and led it to the curb, he pulled in quickly, looked out again just as she was tying the reins to the maple.

Then she stepped out of the shadows and he saw her face.

"Oh, Christ," he groaned, and charged for the door.

FIVE

Lincoln jerked open the shop door just as the woman had raised a not inconsiderable fist to demand entrance. She was startled but not mollified at his prompt, perhaps even preternatural, response to her arrival. A glance to the horse—a magnificent Clydesdale clearly not destined to pull a brewery wagon in anybody's Fourth of July parade —and she strode inside without a word of greeting to lean against one of the display cases, arms folded over her chest while he closed the door, whispered a quick, silent prayer, and switched on the overhead light.

"Hello, Lora," he said somewhat cautiously, mirroring her stance on the other side of the narrow aisle. "What brings you here?"

Loraleen Bannon was Farren Upshire's niece, as well as his trainer, and sometime roustabout when curiosity got the better of people who were not specifically invited to Hillendale. She lived on a dairy farm with her divorced father four miles down the road, a man Linc had never met but who, he had heard from Old Alice, spent most of his spare time trying to figure out a legal way to hold a private lottery which would both marry off his daughter and let him retire without having to clean up after one more cud-dribbling cow. While she was not nearly as overweight as her uncle, she was of recognizably Wagnerian proportions, especially when she wore her jeans tight, her plaid shirt snug and open well below the throat, and her black hair in two braids that thudded down her back to her waist. Generally, and vocally, she distrusted any man who was not capable of shoeing a horse or throwing a hundred-pound bale of hay from one end of the barn to another; generally, she avoided Inverness as a hotbed of prissy civilization and a caldron of unimaginative sin.

And generally, she smiled a lot.

Tonight, however, her expression was stern and her voice deeper than any man's.

"You upset Uncle," she accused.

Lincoln was not intimidated. Loraleen was only nineteen; he'd known her since she was three and knew the size of her diapers. But neither did he want to risk her temper—the last time that had happened, he'd found himself dodging pitchforks and a buckboard just because he wouldn't show her the true meaning of bed and breakfast.

"He upset me," he countered just as sternly. "I don't like being railroaded."

Loraleen's expression told him she had no idea what her uncle was up to, but it was Lincoln's earlier call that had made him so nervous.

"I suppose," he said, "you're going to break both my arms."

"Nope." She reached for her hip pocket.

He tensed, trying to decide which was closer, the front door or the back room. Or maybe it would be better to vault the display case and hope she wouldn't destroy his inventory of handmade shirts and ties. Then he relaxed with an apologetic smile when she handed him an envelope.

"What's this?" The envelope was thick, heavy, and unmarked. "Wait a minute, hold on. I thought we—your uncle and I—had agreed I wouldn't be paid until after I returned with . . . with what he wants."

She shrugged. "I don't know a thing about any payment. All I know is, he sent me to Twainbow's Travel Emporium to pick that up." Her face softened, and when she smiled, it was shyly, almost coyly. "You travel a lot for a tailor, you know? You after some kind of special material for Uncle?"

"You could say that." He held the envelope close to his chest, opened the flap and discovered an airline ticket inside. When he checked the time, he realized he had only three hours to get to Newark Airport, check in, and be on his way. He did not notice that Loraleen had moved to stand beside him and was looking over his shoulder.

"Dallas? Albuquerque? Wow!"

When he glanced up, all he saw was her frontage, which she had thrust none too subtly as close to his face as she had the nerve to, though her eyes suggested that she had more than enough nerve for the both of them.

"I have a message for you," she said huskily.

"I'll bet," he said, easing away toward the back. "Look, I'm in a sudden hurry, Lora. I don't have much—"

"Annabelle is going to meet you at the airport."

He frowned. "Who?"

"Annabelle Bannon. My sister on my mother's side," she said, clearly unhappy at both the relationship and the impending meeting. "She knows what's going on. I don't. Nobody tells me anything. About anything."

A handful of meaningless words of condolence and reassurance were at his lips when, as she moved away from the case, he saw someone standing quietly outside by the Clydesdale. At first he thought it was Carmel, over to yell at him for not joining her cleanup soiree.

A second look told him he was wrong.

It was a man, keeping deep to the maple's shadow, and he was dressed in black.

"Look, Lora," he said, shifting to place her bulk between him and the window, "wait here a minute while I get my bag. There's something I have to—" And he waved the tickets in the air. She nodded as he left, ran upstairs, grabbed his satchel and Alice's money, ran back down and straight into her arms as she started to part the beaded curtain. She grinned and hugged him, and his nose and chin were buried in the canyon between her breasts. It was disconcerting and claustrophobic, though definitely not unpleasant, and he ordered himself to remember her age and the size of her uncle as he pulled away gently, clearing his throat when she slammed an arm solidly around his waist and guided him to the front door.

A poke at the satchel made him freeze at the thought of Palmer's special concoction packed inside.

"You travel light."

He switched off the light.

"Do you . . . I mean . . . like . . . that is . . . I mean, do you ever take anyone with you on one of these things? Like, do you always go alone, when you go?"

"Most of the time," he said. "Like now."

"Oh."

He turned his head away and smiled.

"Y'know," she said, "I forgive you."

"Thanks. About what?"

"About that time in the barn."

"Think nothing of it."

"I've learned a lot since then."

They were outside, and he locked the door behind them. The man in black was gone.

"A lot," she repeated in what she apparently thought was a meaningful tone.

"Good." He looked up and down the street. It was empty save for the couples wandering into Carmel's Shoppe, where the party and its blaring music were going stronger than ever. There were no patrolmen on foot, no late strollers, not even the headlamps of a single car. He wondered where the man had gone, but had no time to sort the possibilities because Loraleen suddenly grabbed him, lifted him, and dumped him on the Clydesdale's back.

"Now wait a minute!"

She swung easily into the saddle behind him, clamped her arms around his waist, and took hold of the reins. "You got to get to the bus station. The bus leaves in ten minutes. I looked. You'll never make it walking."

He looked down at the ground, never thinking an animal could be so high up and still touch bottom. "Lora, please, I'll run. I hate heights."

"I thought you were flying."

"With my eyes closed."

"You're silly, you know that?" and she kissed him wetly on the back of his neck. He squirmed, then gasped as the huge animal lumbered around and started along Creek Road toward the square. Its hooves were extraordinarily loud on the blacktop, echoing off the buildings they passed, and the beast's pitch and roll made him hope its saddle was nailed on.

He was grateful, then, that she held on to him so tightly, but was not so grateful for the streams of warm air steaming the back of his head. Evidently, part of her new education was in advanced heavy breathing, which she'd obviously equated with preparing a lover in a Dutch oven.

The square itself, with its benches, trees, and Revolutionary War monument, passed them on the left, Creek Road continuing around it and up the hill to the Knob where the more well-to-do, including George Vilcroft, had their homes; on the right the road turned a rounded corner and moved down the slope, the shops and municipal buildings giving way to more lawns and houses as the land flattened.

Beyond the winking amber traffic signal at the bottom, the road straightened and vanished into darkness, the only sign that it did continue the rapidly approaching headlamps of what he assumed was a large truck.

Halfway to the next corner, wondering if his back would survive or his loins ever function again, he craned his neck to look behind him.

The only car on the street was just leaving the square.

And its headlamps were out, its engine roaring as it plunged suddenly after them.

Loraleen needed no more than a sudden croaked warning about the driver's intention. She looked, said "Holy Moses on the River Jordan!," and jammed her heels into the horse's sides. The Clydesdale quivered, snorted, tossed its head, and began to run. It was, he thought, like a jumbo jet gathering steam on a muddy runway—the downhill angle helped, but it was still a frustratingly long time before the creature reached speed. Its lurching was less pronounced now, and he was amazed at how fast such a huge animal could go.

He was also amazed at how well it took corners.

At the light, with the menacing car less than twenty yards behind them, Loraleen yanked on the reins and yelled an order, and the horse swerved sharply to the left, directly in front of an eighteen-wheeler whose driver stomped on the brakes just as Lincoln began his final prayer. Loraleen whooped, the airhorn blasted, brakes screamed, and as the truck's right front fender barely skimmed the horse's tail, he could hear the pursuing car braking hard as well.

He didn't dare look. Instead, he grabbed the thick mane more tightly and listened for the accident that did not happen.

The horn's blast faded, the two sets of brakes stopped their protesting, and, except for the Clydesdale's continuing charge, the night was silent.

"Damn, missed him," Loraleen said, guiding her mount to the right side of the road.

He nodded but said nothing. The tail of this Arabian was getting to be a pain in the ass. He also concluded that Upshire could not have entirely been imagining the artifact's powers if so many people were determined to send him after it, and just as many were just as determined to be sure he didn't get it.

He didn't much care about the tail save for what it might do for Farren; right now he was more concerned with leaving New Jersey with his own tail unburned.

Tailors as a folk entity were unassuming and sometimes meek, but Lincoln Bartholomew Blackthorne hated like hell to be pushed around.

"And holy hell in a pulpit, Blackie, we missed it. There's your bus!"

She was right.

Half a mile down the dark road he could see the bus's lights spear at an angle out of the parking lot behind the butcher shop, pausing while it gauged the nonexistent traffic before moving out into its lane.

Damn, he thought; and double damn when he heard the car behind him start another run.

Loraleen, however, swerved the Clydesdale back to the left and turned them around, sped the animal up again, and stared as the bus drove slowly past. It was, she shouted with delight, her old pal Dickie Pell, and he owed her a favor, so hang on, Blackie, because we're gonna catch that bus yet.

The car turned on two wheels, smoke lifting behind it.

Loraleen sent her mount thundering onto the sidewalk where, just before they reached the corner, she plowed them through a man-high hedge that scraped off what Linc thought must have been half the length of his left leg, and charged through a backyard filled with swings and slides and an aboveground swimming pool. The family sitting at the pool's edge waved and laughed and offered them a drink; Linc waved back, and Loraleen shouted that she'd return to fill the divots.

"For god's sake, slow down!" he yelled when he saw the second hedge looming.

"Hot damn and double duty!" she shrieked at the Clydesdale, who tossed its head again, snorted a dozen times, and decided to pretend the hedge didn't exist.

Once through, they were on the west side of the square, and the bus was just coughing its way up the steep slope and around to the other side.

The Clydesdale paced it.

The car came through the hedge behind them.

Loraleen came abreast of the door, reached over, and pounded on the glass.

"Open the damned door, Richard," she screamed, "and let him in!"

Dick Pell looked, blinked, looked away, and looked back.

"Open up, damnit!"

He opened the door, and she grabbed the satchel from Linc's hands and threw it in.

"No!" he pleaded, and "No!" again when she lifted him one-handed from the saddle and dumped him in the stairwell. He grabbed the slickly polished handrail and sagged, watching fearfully as she dropped back and swerved with a whoop to force the pursuing car over the curb and up the courthouse steps, where it came to a stop against a pedestal holding a green-faced statue of Blind Justice.

A policeman was having a cigarette in the doorway. When the car stopped, Linc could have sworn the cop smiled as he reached for his gun.

"Hey!"

He turned in a crouch, one hand reaching for his gun, the other for his cosh.

Dick Pell held out a hand.

"You owe me five bucks. Where you going?"

Lincoln staggered up the steps and retrieved the satchel. Then he dropped into the front seat and wiped his face with one arm. He was, he thought, a better packer than he knew. "Newark Airport."

"I don't go there."

Linc reached into his pocket and pulled out his wallet. "How close do you get?" He handed the man a twenty.

"A mile or two."

Another twenty.

Pell looked into the back of the bus. It was empty.

Another twenty.

"What airline?"

"American."

"I'll drop you at your seat."

He swayed to the back seat, stretched out, and looked through the window. Loraleen was standing on the curb beside the Clydesdale, the dark car was losing steam through its grille, and the policeman was talking animatedly with the man in black. Just as the bus swung around the corner and coughed into high gear, the policeman pointed, and the man in black turned, and smiled right at Lincoln.

SIX

The plane shuddered through some minor turbulence, and Lincoln gripped his thighs tightly. It's going to be all right, he thought; just like riding over potholes five miles deep.

A sickly smile at the stewardess who'd been winking at him the entire flight, and he ordered himself to think about something else. He had, however, already gone over everything a dozen times, rehashing and reexamining Upshire's claim about the gold-threaded talisman, and Vilcroft's apparent willingness to go along with such a literally fantastic notion.

Skepticism, he knew, was healthy, but experiences he really had not gone in search of had also taught him that belief was equal to a long and healthy life.

He had, on many previous occasions over the past decade or so, heard and been witness to what anyone else in the civilized world would run to the nearest priest or shrink for; he had been threatened by, terrified of, and nearly killed by that which had previously only been the province of special effects men in not so special films. Though he had never seen a demon or battled with Satan or cast or seen cast anything like a magic spell, there were too many times when what he heard and was witness to came too damned close for comfort to what a sane man would call the results of a vivid nightmare.

And there were times when others, unlike Farren Upshire, sought the same things for purposes not exactly conducive to the good night's sleep of the world.

Lincoln did not believe in saving the universe.

He did believe in saving his own skin.

To that end he squirmed a bit in his seat and glanced casually over his shoulder, to a rear seat on the lefthand side, to an arm wearing a black sleeve. He might have been mistaken, but he knew he wasn't. There weren't too many shirtsleeves like that—black silk, wide french cuffs, and the cufflinks silver and in the image of a skull.

Because of a large woman sitting on the aisle behind him, he could not see the man in black's face, but he was more than a little annoyed that he'd not been able to shake him. It was going to make things much more difficult when they finally landed. What he could not understand was why the man, after trying so openly to kill him back in Inverness, hadn't tried anything since. There had certainly been enough opportunities—the flight to Dallas, Dallas itself and the hours waiting until dawn for the next flight west, and here on the plane itself.

It was as if, having failed once, the man was gun-shy.

Or, he thought, he'd had further instructions.

The plane shuddered again, and he swallowed hard, hoping the pilot understood the distress he was causing. Then he scowled at himself. That wasn't really fair. He hadn't objected strenuously to the flight to Dallas since, whenever he could bring himself to look out the window, all he could see was the black of night below him, and a few concentrations of light that marked a passing town. From Dallas to Albuquerque, on the other hand, the brown, flat, uninspiring landscape was totally visible, and he was able to pick out any number of spots where the plane and its all too vulnerable cargo, when it and they went down, could easily smash into innumerable pieces.

How in god's name something from the butt end of a mythical Arabian horse had found its way out here was beyond him.

A dip for a downdraft, and he discovered the perfect spot where search parties would never find them.

Worse, however, was when the land changed.

The brown became desert spotted with lonely patches of green, and as far as he could tell, there wasn't a single human being alive down there; then the desert began to climb, isolated mountain ranges breaking the monotony of the tabletop land, their isolation ending when, just as the pilot suggested his passengers prepare themselves for the descent, he could see directly ahead the slopes leading to the peaks of the Sandia Mountains, ten thousand feet about sea level, five thousand feet above the city to which he was traveling.

And their peaks were buried in ugly grey cloud.

People began to shift in anticipation; the engines began to roar, and he decided that doing something about the man in black couldn't wait any longer. After taking a deep breath to bring him some calm, he unbuckled his seat belt and moved into the aisle. He took a deliberate moment to make a show of stretching and fiddling with his belt, then shook his head as if embarrassed at himself before walking to the forward rest rooms, grimacing urgently when the stewardess made to gesture him back to his place. Quickly, he opened the center door, stepped into the cubicle, and closed but did not lock it. Then he stood on the stainless toilet seat and waited.

Less than a minute later there was a tentative knock, and when there was no answer, the man in black sidled in.

Lincoln smiled at him, and suggested with the barrel of the gun Palmer had given him that he close and lock the door. The man did. Then he requested that the man turn around and place his hands high on the walls on either side of the entrance. He did. And Lincoln puffed his cheeks in relief.

The man in black was a virtual twin of the man in white—the same skeletal face and the same stringy, dead-looking hair. The only difference was, now he could see the color of the deep-set eyes—they were as black as his hair, and just as lifeless.

"If you shoot," the man said, his voice toneless, "you'll puncture the skin of the plane and we'll go down."

"If I shoot," Lincoln told him, "the bullet will go no farther than your spine, I promise you."

The plane dipped and rocked, and so did Lincoln's stomach and his perch on the toilet.

"I suppose it'd be useless to ask who you work for."

The man in black nodded. Once. Slowly.

He stepped down to the floor and rammed the barrel into the man's back. "And I suppose it would be just as useless to ask why you tried to kill me back there."

Again the nod.

And the man in black kicked suddenly back, catching Lincoln on the shin with the heel of his boot. Linc grunted and tottered, the toilet catching his calves as the man whirled and snared his gunhand while his free hand immediately went for his throat.

The eyes were still lifeless, and the bloodless lips were pulled back to expose a set of perfectly even, stained yellow teeth.

Lincoln brought his knee up, but it was diverted by a thigh; he tried to twist to one side, but the grip on his throat was losing him air, and being bent backward as he was, his head hard against the wall, his attempt to squirm into a more tenable position was next to impossible.

The black eyes stared.

Lincoln's vision blurred as he strained to free the gun.

The gun wavered in the air, pointing at the ceiling and making Linc's hopes of using it less than zero. But he tried to bring it against the man's temple, his arm straining while his mouth opened wide to gulp for air.

The black eyes moved closer.

Then, as his vision began to fill with swarming motes of grey in a faint red haze, he suddenly lifted his feet and dropped onto the toilet. The man in black was pitched forward, his forehead cracking against the wall, stunning him just long enough for Linc to thrust him to one side, put a boot hard into the small of his back, and listen for the sound of the man's spine cracking in half.

It didn't happen.

Instead, the man groaned, trying to clutch his back and his head at the same time. He groaned louder, then hissed and staggered to his feet, any thought of attacking again gone when Linc pulled back the hammer and pointed the barrel straight at the middle of his forehead.

"Who, and why?" he demanded in a hoarse voice, his throat stinging as if coated with acid.

Though still somewhat groggy, the man in black managed a mirthless smile.

Well, that's fair enough, he thought, and waved at the man to turn around, tapped his upper arms to have him bring his hands behind his back. When he did, after a second prodding, Linc took off the man's snakeskin belt and tied them swiftly and intricately, keeping the gun barrel in the man's neck as a reminder. Once done, he examined the knot, wondered why a man would wear a belt like that, and saw the "Take Your Seat" sign flashing overhead. With a smile of his own he maneuvered his prisoner around and pushed him down onto the seat.

The man in black, his high forehead already sporting a knobbed bruise, grinned. "I can get out, you know."

"I know. But not for a while."

"You're a fool, Blackthorne. You're going to die."

"Maybe," he said. "But not in a bathroom."

"I am," he said, still grinning, still in a voice that sounded like the grave, "an adept at escape."

Lincoln didn't hesitate to believe him, and in believing him had no compunctions when he brought the gun barrel down on the side of the man's head. Then he left, turned and closed the door, adjusted his clothes, and reeled back to his seat.

Once he was buckled in again, he looked out the window and almost gasped aloud. He stopped the stewardess and pointed. "Where is the airport?" he said anxiously.

"Over there," she told him, leaning across two empty seats to accommodate him. "On the other side of the mountains."

"But you can't see the tops. Does he go around?"

"Nope," she said. "Right over. See, the airport's not all that far away. He has to start dropping about . . . oh, about now."

"Blind."

"Don't worry. There are instruments."

"Like for finding metal?"

She grinned, patted his cheek in a motherly fashion, and continued on up the aisle. He watched as she spoke softly with another passenger, reminded still another to raise the seatback upright, and knocked on the three rest room doors, her head tilted to listen for a response. He held his breath. She tried each of the doors to be sure they were secure. He frowned. She opened one, another, and was reaching for a third when the pilot's voice came over the intercom and asked them all to be seated.

Thank you, he thought, and changed his mind when the clouds obscured his vision of the outside world, and he instantly began his own peculiar ritual of guiding the plane in with a bit of body english and stomping on the floor as if he had brakes.

The plane jumped, bucked, and dropped in time to the revolutions of his stomach.

The clouds thickened.

He wondered how close the peaks were, remembered how high they rose over the desert floor, and decided as the windows streaked with rain that he didn't want to know.

Then the airliner banked sharply to the right, came about, and banked left. In less than an eyeblink they were in the open, Albuquerque spread out below them from the foot of the mountains into the desert south and west. He was so relieved he didn't think about it as he examined the city, the downtown notable as far as he could tell for being the only place in the sprawling city with buildings taller than four or five stories, and there were so few of them that they were gone by the time he realized they were there in the first place.

Another bank, wobbling and too sharp, and a number of people swore loudly. He checked the rest room door; it was still closed, and none of the stewardesses were anywhere near it.

The city vanished, and they were over desert again, until the engines rushed and whined and the plane bounced on a runway he hadn't noticed approaching. It bounced a second time, a third, and five minutes later they were at the terminal.

Two minutes after that, and after tromping on a number of toes, he was in the jetway with his satchel, praying that the other passengers would be, as usual, poking and scrambling into the overhead compartments for whatever they had carried on board. He figured on three, maybe four minutes before the man in black would be able to catch up with him, assuming he'd revive about the time of the landing.

That left him about thirty seconds to find Annabelle Bannon.

The moment he stepped into the waiting room, however, he stopped, looked around, and wondered if he were in an airport or a chapel for disaster victims.

The room was not large, most of it taken up by long churchlike pews filled with those waiting to depart and those waiting for those arriving—most of them unquestionably of either Indian or Mexican descent, the rest Anglo tourists in cowboy hats, boots, and jeans, or locals in cowboy hats, boots, and jeans.

On the right were two airline counters and a lunchstand, on the left a crowded gift shop that as far as he could tell sold only mugs, T-shirts, and Indian jewelry. Voices were loud, not all of them speaking English, and he wanted to stop someone and ask if he was really in New Mexico's largest city and not a border town where they frisked you and your horse before giving you passage.

He never had the chance.

A woman stepped up to him, threw her arms around his neck, and whispered in his ear: "I have a knife. Don't scream or I'll take off your scalp."

SEVEN

After what had happened in the airplane, and with little time left to make his escape, Lincoln had little tolerance left for any delays. He looked down at the woman still clinging to his neck and said, "Do you mind?"

She frowned, leaned her head back and stared at him, blinking. "I said I had a knife."

"I heard you the first time."

"But that's supposed to be the password. Aren't you Lincoln Blackthorne?"

"I am," he said in a whisper, and with a furtive glance behind him at the chattering, waving passengers trailing out of the jetway. An old woman beamed at him, the quintessential grandmother enjoying the tender reunion, and he smiled back, nodding as if to say, *it's been a long time, ma'am, and we got a lotta catchin' up t'do.* Then carefully, so as not to attract the attention of the old woman, or the potbellied representative of airport security who might think he was being a little disrespectful to the local female population, he disengaged her arms and walked her hurriedly through the crowd to the escalators on the far side of the room. "And you must be Annabelle Bannon."

"Right! But why didn't you answer me? Didn't Loraleen give you the password?" She held up a hand to forestall response. "No, never mind. Obviously, she didn't. The little creep. She's always doing that, you know. All her life she's been a real pain in— Hey, buddy, watch where you're going!" she snapped at a young man who skipped away from the well-aimed point of her boot, clearing the escalator's entrance and allowing them to descend.

Annabelle remained in front, and Lincoln watched her as she complained about how they had to traipse halfway across the state just to get their luggage, which wouldn't be there anyway, so what's the big hurry.

She was his height, perhaps an inch shorter, with short black hair brushed back over her ears. Her figure was slight in shirt and jeans, and he could not see an extraneous ounce of fat on her anywhere. Her face and hands were deeply tanned, her eyes when he saw them as dark as her hair, and her mouth though wide showed no teeth when she smiled.

"Why the big rush?" she asked in annoyance when he took her arm at the elbow and rushed them along the tiled corridor. "I told you the bags wouldn't be there, didn't I? They work on it, you know. They take lessons on how to unload planes with their teeth and their toes. I think they have a record book somewhere they're trying to get into, if you know what I mean."

"I'm anxious for the tour, and I have my bag right here," he said, and looked over his shoulder.

She caught the look, followed it down the hall, and broke into a trot. "Okay," and he knew instantly that she had read his mind.

In less than two minutes they were outside, and he was holding his chest and gasping. "Good lord, I thought New Mexico was comfortable in June."

He had been told not to worry about the heat; no matter how high the temperature, it was only dry desert air and more or less bearable despite the time of year. What he hadn't been told about, and which Annabelle told him now with what he thought was rather undue glee, was the city's elevation—five thousand air-thinning feet above sea level, which added greatly to the heat and sapped him instantly. His sinuses felt as though they'd packed up and gone back East, his skin was ready to peel off in layers, and when he took a deep breath, he didn't feel a thing.

"Comfortable? For who?" she said, pulling him across the parking lot to a large white Cadillac convertible at least twenty years old. "Roadrunners and coyotes like it, I guess, and a few idiots who come here on their pensions because they think it's healthier than Chicago."

She flung the satchel into the back seat, looked at his panicked expression with a frown, and vaulted over the door, waving him to join her because she wasn't waiting for clearance from the tower. Before he was fully seated, she was weaving expertly through the lanes to the pay booth, threw a dollar at the attendant, and barely missed clipping off the barrier.

He checked behind; no one was following. He looked front, and decided he'd rather get back on the plane.

Annabelle was jockeying with the rest of the city's equally heedless drivers for the single best position on the highway where driving was fast and easy, and concentration was at its lowest. She said nothing, just pointed east toward the looming mountains, and once on the six-lane interstate that cut through the town, she pushed down the accelerator as far as it would go.

"Who is he?" she asked with mild interest as she jerked a thumb over her shoulder.

"I don't know his name."

"Does he want to kill us?"

"Could be," he said, checking again. "He tried once. So did a buddy of his."

"Does Uncle Farren know about this?"

"To tell you the truth, I don't know," he said over the rush of the wind. "About the first guy, yes. About this other one, I'm not sure."

She dodged a police car with its red lights spinning, a van with a surfboard strapped to the top, and a battered station wagon from the university. "He probably doesn't. All he thinks about are those damned fool horses of his."

He was surprised. "You don't like horses?"

She gave him a withering look that shut him up, and he crouched lower into the white leather seat, hoping the hot wind spilling over the windshield wouldn't blast away every hair from his head.

"Y'know, I think I'm going to kill Loraleen for that stupid password trick," she said after five minutes of silence. "Do you know I must have hugged at least fifteen guys in that place? I kid you not—fifteen of them. I could have made a fortune, actually, if I was that kind of woman and not very choosy. You can smoke if you want to."

He declined, and looked the other way as she fumbled in her shirt pocket for a cigarette and decided to forego the convenience of the car's lighter for the one in her jeans, which required her to lift half out of her seat in order to free it so she could use it.

"Nice place," he said finally, swallowing his terror and looking around. "Sort of spread out like Los Angeles."

"Yeah. Nice, if you like anthills."

The city swept past them faster than he would like—low stucco houses buried beneath high-crowned trees and hidden behind walls painted to look like adobe, sprawling shopping centers here and there, hotels with their names garish in red neon, step-back and boxy condominiums and apartment complexes that crawled toward the slopes of the Sandias, which themselves seemed to rise straight up from the desert floor—jagged, patched with greens and browns, split by canyons no self-respecting burro would want to call home. At the top he could see a handful of television towers, what might have been an observation deck, and a lone hang glider swooping low over it all with the grace of an eagle.

Every so often he saw what looked like large ditches sided in concrete splitting developments, neighborhoods, once even a small business office complex. When he asked, she told him they were once arroyos, and when it rained in the mountains they still carried water. Not for long, however; flash flooding only, and more than once a child playing there had been caught and drowned by the rushing water. When he commented on the clouds still hovering over the peaks, and on those billowing white and grey several miles up in an apparent effort to surround the city, she laughed and slapped the steering wheel.

"They're like men," she said with a sardonic grin. "They promise, but they seldom deliver."

"How wonderful for you." He looked again at a concrete-sided arroyo. "And I suppose you have earthquakes on weekends, just for fun."

"Sure," she said blithely. "Not big, but they're here. Like men, they make you shake a little, but that's all."

"Don't you like men, either?" he said, thinking this was going to be one wonderful trip.

"Sure," she said, and looked him over carefully, slowly, so slowly that he had to point at the road to redirect her attention. "I like them. I just don't trust them very much."

"Present company included?"

"We'll see," she said. "We'll see."

"Nice," he said.

"Don't worry about it," she told him. "I don't trust women, either. They like men too much."

"Is there anybody you do like?"

"I'm working on it," she said, and her lips almost parted in the ghost of a grin.

The interstate angled smoothly to the right, where the Sandias stopped just long enough for it to pass through.

The city fell behind them as they passed between the walls of what she told him was Tijeras Canyon, with sagebrush, low pine, and other desert shrubs poking through the ground where it wasn't split by dry riverbeds that hadn't seen a drop of water since Coronado and his army tramped through on their way to El Dorado; and what few streams were still full had their erratic courses marked by dense concentrations of trees and grass that almost glowed so startlingly intense was their green against the drab hillsides. There were a few pockets of homes, what looked to be a ghost town it seemed so uninviting, and a larger community whose name flashed by so fast he couldn't catch it when they left the highway for a two-lane road.

"Where are we going?" he asked when they finally slowed down to something more like sixty than ninety.

"My place—the ranch, that is—is between here and Santa Fe," she said. "We could have gone the other way, around the other side of the mountains on the interstate, but this way is shorter."

Slower still as they left the Sandias behind them and another range, even higher, climbed into view ahead.

"Did . . . have you talked with your uncle?" he asked as he pushed himself into the corner of the seat, the better to see her reaction, and to watch the road behind.

They were, for the time being, alone, the sun climbing toward noon and not a cloud left in the sky save for those few clinging stubbornly to the mountaintops. A dim flash of lightning; a distant rumbling of thunder.

They were alone, and the silence of it, the expanse of it with not another soul in sight, began to work on his nerves. Though he lived in a small town and groused constantly about its growing, he was still used to the proximity of people. This, on the other hand, was something he had seldom experienced—virtually complete desolation, in the middle of the twentieth century, and he didn't like it one bit. He knew that if he didn't keep talking, he'd soon be seeing murderous shadows where no shadows existed.

He asked her again about talking with Farren.

She nodded. "He called me just after you left. In what I gather was something of an event back there in Jersey."

An image of the huffing, charging Clydesdale came to mind, and he nodded. "It was your sister's idea, actually. I'm a bit more conservative. To say the least, it was an unusual departure." Another image of the man in black in his lightless car, and the impulse to smile faded. "So what did he say?"

"He told me everything."

From the tone of her voice, he knew he was in trouble. "And?"

"He's nuts."

"He believes it, Annabelle."

She shook her head, her expression somewhat surprisingly both sad and bitter. "If you told a fat man he was going to die in six months unless he ate nothing but refried beans and stale burritos, he'd believe it."

"I believe him."

A curve in the road took her attention, and when they were out of it, they were crossing flatland ringed in the distance by the ever-present mountains. He could see that most of the land on both sides was fenced off with barbed wire, and a few head of cattle roamed the dry riverbeds.

"Then you're as crazy as he is."

This wasn't trouble, he amended; this was pure and simple, out-and-out disaster.

"I tried to tell him that this wouldn't do him any good, but he wouldn't listen." Her voice almost broke, and she gripped the wheel more tightly. "He's nuts. You're nuts. This whole thing is absolutely crazy."

"Then why did you pick me up?"

"Well, one reason is that Loraleen got on the line and told me to keep my hands off you because you were her guy. And I never, Mr. Blackthorne, but never do anything Loraleen tells me."

He sifted through the words for anything he might construe as a compliment, gave up, and wondered how in hell Farren expected him to do anything when not even his own family was willing to lend him a hand.

"What's the other reason?"

"Me."

"Ah. Family loyalty?"

"Not a bit of it," she told him coldly. "Don't kid yourself, Blackthorne."

He lay his arm across the back of the seat and drummed thoughtfully. "I'm sorry," he said, giving up all pretense of politeness. "I thought you were close to your uncle. He certainly gave me that impression."

Inexplicably, she laughed, so hard that tears sparkled on her cheeks until she shook them angrily away. The convertible swerved dangerously. The road gave them no quarter.

"Well, you've been honest with me, so I'll be honest with you, Lincoln. Can I call you Lincoln? Loraleen told me I should call you Blackie. I have a feeling that's another one of her stupid password-type jokes." She smiled, tentatively, groped for another cigarette, and changed her mind. "You're going to find out anyway, so I might as well tell you now that when Uncle Farren dies, I'll inherit the farm.

"I see," he muttered, seeing it clearly long before she decided to continue.

"So my thinking is, I'll kill you, Uncle Farren will die, and I'll be so damned rich I can get out of this godforsaken place."

He pushed closer to the door. "Kill me?"

"Sure," she said, and reached across him to pull a revolver from the glove compartment. "Shoot you, leave you in the desert, and by tomorrow morning there won't be anything left of you but a pile of bones."

"Oh," he said.

"Right," she said, and pulled the trigger.

EIGHT

He had tensed to lunge across the seat in what he knew would be a futile attempt to deflect her aim, and barely caught himself when she swung the barrel over her shoulder instead and fired at the red pickup closing on them rapidly. She hadn't a hope of hitting it, but the shot served its purpose—the truck veered wildly across the road, recovered and dropped back, and Lincoln closed his eyes in relief, not bothering to ask why she'd done it; he knew the answer as soon as the driver, who was hidden by the sun's glare on his windshield, stuck his left hand out the window and fired back.

"Jealous boyfriend?" he asked hopefully.

Three more shots missed, another took off the side mirror, and a sixth he felt buzz by his ear on its way to shattering the face of the radio.

"Now that," Annabelle said disgustedly, "is a crime. That was original equipment."

"So is this," he said, tapping his chest sincerely, just over his heart.

For an answer she dropped the gun in his lap and concentrated on her driving. The truck, no longer threatened by answering fire, closed the gap with a roar and slammed into their rear bumper. The driver was still invisible, but Linc knew who it was, and knew that it was past time to stop behaving like a gentleman. He aimed carefully at the place where the man's head would be and pulled the trigger.

Nothing happened.

He pulled the trigger again, and a third time, then stared at it in disgust. "Hey, it's supposed to have six shots!"

"Well," she said with an apologetic shrug, "I'm really not too keen on guns. I figure one shot will scare anyone away."

"Nice," he said, gripping the padded dashboard as the truck rammed them again.

His head snapped back, and the convertible slewed across the blacktop, over a low rise and down again. There was no oncoming traffic, but neither were there any side roads they could take to attempt an escape across country. When with a shout he asked about the next real turn that might take them back toward the city where they might get hold of a cop, she looked at him oddly and told him that if he was really interested, it was up past the state penitentiary, some forty miles away.

"Hell of a place you have here," he muttered, peering over the back of his seat.

"No place to go to, why should there be roads?" she said. "And the nearest town now is Golden, a few miles up and mostly shacks, trailers, and an abandoned mine."

The pickup, its battering-ram technique failing, tried to muscle over to the left and drive them onto the narrow shoulder, but Annabelle blocked him neatly and took off the spiked green heads of a hundred yards of new tumbleweed in the process. By the time they were back on the road, the truck had surged parallel to their right rear tire, and Lincoln finally caught a glimpse of the driver before the Cadillac drew away.

The man in black nodded.

Lincoln nodded back.

The convertible spurted forward, and the engine began to whine, the frame shimmied, and he couldn't believe there was no one else on the road, no houses or diners to stop at to call the police. They might as well have been on the moon for all the support they were getting.

He looked to Annabelle then and saw the white-knuckled grip she had on the steering wheel, the perspiration that ran freely down the sides of her face. Her hair was already matted to her scalp, and her lips moved as if she were cursing, or praying.

He patted her shoulder once, and she gave him a quick, grateful smile filled with apprehension.

With his hands fisted in helplessness, he couldn't stop himself from looking back, watching the red vehicle pace them fifty yards away. The man in black seemed to sense something and was waiting, and Linc checked the barren roadside for signs of impending disaster—a rickety bridge they'd have to cross, a construction site that would slow them down—and why the hell hadn't he fired again?

Because, you jackass, an accident looks better.

The Cadillac sputtered.

"Hell," he muttered.

Annabelle punched at the steering wheel and whimpered her frustration as the car slowed in spite of her foot punching at the pedal. A desperate look to him, and he thought she was going to cry.

Then the truck rammed them again, and they were out of control.

The car shuddered violently under the impact, and he knew instantly from the sound of the engine and the protesting tires what was going to happen.

There was nothing he could do. Nothing at all.

With a hand on the door then, and the other on the dashboard, he braced himself while they slewed wildly back and forth over the blacktop, Annabelle struggling to find the direction of the skid while panicked about the location of the accelerator and brake. It took longer than he expected, but they were soon careening along the left shoulder, bouncing over rocks, depressions, and flattening sagebrush and yucca. A storm of dust whipped over the hood and darkened the windshield, slipped into his eyes, and made him throw up an arm to protect his face.

The car had slowed considerably, but not nearly enough.

A moment then when he thought he was nestled back in the airplane, soaring peacefully out of Dallas, quietly, not a care in the world; another when he felt his stomach lodge permanently in his throat. And when the car hit, he heard Annabelle scream once, heard himself swear as he was thrown over the windshield, the hood, and a struggling piñon tree less than a yard high.

He landed on his back, twisted and rolled with the direction as far as his momentum could take him, which was down a pock-walled arroyo where he finally came up against a large clot of dirt that shattered on impact.

His first thought was: Wonderful, I'm still alive.

His breath was gone. He wheezed as he lay there, staring at a sky too bright to look at, spitting dust and dry grass from his mouth, and waiting for the fire in his shoulders and right leg to subside. He felt as though razors and dull blades were being tested on his skin, yet there was no immediate sensation of blood or broken bone.

Once the roaring left his ears, he heard nothing but his own lungs creaking back into shape, and he saw nothing until he raised his head and looked straight into the barrel of a reconditioned Colt .45.

"You ain't dead," the man in black said gleefully. "Guess I'll have to fix that."

Lincoln pushed himself painfully onto his elbows, shifting to keep the sun behind the man's head. Dust sifted down the arroyo's steep pitted slope, and from a spot to his right he could hear the groaning of metal as the convertible cooled down. He could not hear Annabelle.

The man in black smiled by pulling back his lips to expose his teeth; nothing else moved on his pale scarred face.

"Worried about the girl?"

He nodded, not knowing if he could speak without squeaking.

"Hell of a bump on her head, that's all."

"No thanks to you," he said at last.

The man laughed, a gasping sound that made Linc look away; it sounded too much like too many death rattles he'd heard.

The Colt's hammer was thumbed back.

Linc shifted again, grimacing at the complaining his back was doing. "You mind telling me who you work for, at least?"

The man in black chuckled. "No you don't, Blackthorne. You ain't gonna get me talking so you can figure a way out of this. I'm too smart for that. Time is not something I have a lot of right now, so you can just lie back there like a good little tailor and take your medicine like a man."

"That's sort of a mixed metaphor, isn't it?"

The man closed one eye to think about it, and Linc lashed out with his left foot to crack his heel against the man's knee. As he did, he rolled over, and when the gun went off, he wasn't where he was supposed to be. Then he was on his feet and running, head down, directly into the man's stomach. The revolver's butt slammed onto his spine before they both fell, and he grunted, snapping up the heel of his hand into the man's bony chin, while the other fist caught him flush on the cheek and whipped his head back against the dirt wall.

Like climbing a ladder of grease-covered snakes, he scrambled until they were wrestling face-to-face, kicking the air, groping blindly for each other's throats, doing more damage to the riverbed than to each other. The gun was gone, and Linc made no attempt to locate it; the moment he lost his concentration he knew he was dead.

The man in black tried to bring a knee into Linc's groin, and caught his hip instead; Linc tried butting his eyes or his nose; the man clamped his hands on either side of Linc's head and squeezed until Linc felt himself tottering on the threshold of unconsciousness; he grabbed the wrists and pulled them apart, rocked onto his back and brought his knees into the man's stomach; the man in black bared his teeth and aimed for Linc's neck; Linc pushed and released his grip, and the man tumbled backward, twisting neatly into a perfect somersault that brought him upright, right next to the gun.

Oh, great, Linc thought, and jumped to a crouch, flexed the muscles of his right forearm and watched in dismay as his knife sprang from its sheath, missed his closing fingers and buried itself blade down almost ten feet away.

Great, he thought again, scooped up a handful of dirt and flung it into the man's eyes, spun around and ran, not forgetting to snatch up the knife and curse it and Palmer soundly while he slipped it back into place.

This time, instead of trying to take the man again, he headed down the twisting arroyo which wound away from the road in such serpentine convolutions that there were never more than ten or fifteen feet between outcroppings, thus keeping him out of the

Colt's direct sights. He had no idea where he was going, but the sound of pursuit was sufficient to prevent him trying to climb out of the dead river—the earth was too loose, brown and clay red, and when he thought about using as steps the many holes he saw there, he changed his mind when he spotted the dim form of a snake just inside one of the openings.

There were a lot of things he hadn't been told about this place he'd been sent to; if he found something else, he was going to scream.

The riverbed forked, and he picked a direction blindly; it forked again a few minutes later, and he wasted no time tossing a coin.

The man in black fired once, there was no echo, and no dirt was kicked up.

It was a deliberate prod; Linc knew the tactic, and still he ran—through sharp-edged grass, through brittle shrubs that tore at his jeans as he passed, around the bones of a small animal, around the bones of something larger.

He ran, and he sweated, and before long the weight of his legs and the shallow working of his lungs pulled him into a crouch that caused him to stumble, set hazy spirals of faint red in front of his eyes and made his head ache.

He slowed.

He turned as he moved to chance a look behind him, almost smiling when he saw nothing back there but what lay ahead.

He tripped over a rock and couldn't get his hands out fast enough to break his fall. He landed clumsily on his right shoulder, skidded a foot or two on his cheek before toppling onto his back, and was tempted to let himself drift off—to hide the pain, to escape the heat, to be unconscious when the man in black caught up with him and did it at last.

He lay there for several minutes.

Nothing happened.

A gallant gesture, he thought as he struggled to his hands and knees; the man did his best, but he came up short, unprepared for the altitude and the terrain.

He stood and tilted his head, opened his mouth, and gulped for air; hands gripped his waist, and he turned slowly to face the direction he'd just left.

A fly explored his face, and large red ants marched over his boots until he crushed them with a mirthless smile.

A large bird glided in wide circles overhead, too high for him to make out details, too low for comfort if it was something like a vulture.

He waited for another five minutes before he realized there was no one there, and no one was coming. It was too soon to celebrate, and he was too sore to click his heels, but he allowed himself a satisfied smile and a deep breath before deciding he'd best start back for Annabelle or, at the least, to find the road. And after that a long, sinfully long shower, something cool to drink, and then he was going to beat the hell out of someone unless someone explained to him what the hell was going on.

Wary of treading on scorpions, rattlers, or anything else that might attack without asking questions first, he found a clear section of wall and dragged himself out of the arroyo. And knew with a glance why the man in black had chosen not to follow.

There were mountains behind him, larger mountains far ahead, and other than that he couldn't see a thing save for New Mexico's high desert.

"Why that sonofabitch," he said. "He lost me."

Literally.

Always keeping the riverbed in sight, he walked several paces in all directions, trying to find a hint of a highway or a sign of habitation. But there was nothing out there. No smoke, no road noise, not even a bird singing.

He was disgusted with himself—for being herded away from safety as though he were some fool amateur, for not jumping the man in black instead of running away, for not doing *something* to mark his escape route so he could follow it back. All that was rudimentary, and he hadn't done a thing.

Kicking angrily at the ground, he stalked to a low piñon tree with a multitude of twisted thin trunks that held a rich crown of still green leaves. At least it would give him shade, and after a moment's thought he climbed into it, as high as he could in the futile hope he might be able to see something important.

He was fifteen feet up, and saw nothing at all.

On the way down, however, he did.

A rattlesnake waited at the base of the tree, coiled, head high, and its rattles loud and angry.

NINE

It was the largest snake Lincoln had seen without leaving the country, and the way he felt now, it could well have been the largest he'd ever seen in his life. On television they didn't look nearly so thick around the middle, nor did their eyes resemble such hard, malevolent gemstones, nor were those rattles so infernally loud. It was, he admitted, a strikingly beautiful creature in its own evil way, and at any other time he would have been grateful for the opportunity to study it more closely.

However, there were problems.

First, despite the relatively cool shade the tree offered him, the early afternoon sun was growing stronger, which in turn made him thirsty, which reminded him that he hadn't had a thing to eat or drink since leaving Dallas a hundred years ago. At the suggestion, his stomach began to grumble, and his throat and tongue felt coated with an inch of grating dust. He supposed he could chew on the piñon needles, but he might as well be in Peru for all he knew about the dangers of the local flora, and with the snake down below that was a risk he wasn't willing to take.

Second, he could always jump down on the other side and hope the rattler was only making noises, defending its territory and unhappy about his intrusion. With him gone and the potential danger over, it might well slither off to wherever snakes slither off to and carry on with its life.

On the other hand, it might not.

It might decide to come after him, and he had no idea how fast those things could travel. The way he felt now, if it moved any faster than a dead man's crawl, he'd be bitten before he'd taken five steps.

Which was the third thing—he was hurting worse than ever. His leg was acting up again, and when he prodded calf and shin, he bit back a gasp; the muscle was badly strained, and it could very well be torn. And half sitting, half standing here in this impossible tree was not doing the rest of him much good either. Cramps were going to be a definite threat, and one slip would put him right in the rattler's lap.

And, he thought, thinking of a fourth thing which he certainly didn't need to think of, even if he was able to get away, where would he go? He was still lost, and he imagined that where there was one desert predator there was probably another.

It occurred to him then that sitting here in the tree wasn't the worst thing that could happen. And if he stuck around until nightfall, there was a good chance he might be able to spot the glow of headlamps on the road, thus giving him a direction, and something a lot safer to walk on than the desert floor.

"So," he said to the snake, who was still coiled but noiseless, "what's your name?"

The rattles started again.

He grinned, then yelped and yanked himself higher when the snake struck upward, narrowly missing his heel.

"Lord," he whispered.

The snake coiled again, and rattled. Its tongue flicked out ceaselessly, testing the air.

A bee hovered in front of his face, and he nearly laughed aloud at the mundane menace.

That hawk or buzzard or whatever it was was still up there, still circling, dipping, circling again.

The snake had quieted, but it hadn't moved.

He examined the tree's bark, studied a needle, closed one eye and looked at the sky, closed the other and tried to devise experiments to test his depth perception. Then he looked down and knew his luck was holding—the snake wasn't alone. Now there were two, and as he watched them swarming over each other, a third one crawled up, much smaller, with fewer rattles on its tail, and just as mean-looking as either of its brothers.

Then the thin branch he was leaning against snapped under the continuous pressure of his weight.

He yelled and flailed as he fell, barely managing to grab hold before he hit ground, less than two feet between him and the three snakes, who were all coiled now and rattling so hard he could hear nothing else. He was within easy striking range of even the smallest, and as he tried to haul himself back up, he felt a thud against his boot, a second soon following, and a third, and he held his breath, waiting for the pain, for the paralysis to make him lose his grip and fall.

And when nothing happened, he brought his left foot slowly up to brace it against the trunk. A look, and he saw a row of faint indentations where their fangs had tried to puncture the thick heel, and a glinting strand of milky liquid where the remains of their venom still dripped.

He closed his eyes and swallowed.

He opened them again when someone said, "Don't move."

And closed them a second time when a shotgun went off.

When he didn't immediately die and wasn't shredded with pellets, he looked under his arm and saw a man standing alone, a few feet to his left. He was tall and slender, his straight black hair parted in the center and just touching his shoulders. A beaded sweatband split his dark forehead, his shirt and trousers were loose to allow the circulation of air, and on his feet was a pair of raw leather boots laced up to a fringe just below his knees. A shotgun was cradled in his arms, and he was reloading without taking his gaze from the remains of the rattlesnakes now scattered over twenty feet of desert ground.

"You going to stay up there all day?"

Lincoln did not think his arms would work, and he was surprised to find himself on the ground again, gingerly stepping over the bloody snakes to shake the man's hand.

"I'm—"

"Yeah," said the man. "And I'm Peter Wolf."

Linc wanted to say something more, but a roiling cloud of dizziness interrupted him, and the next thing he knew he was lying on his back, something folded under his head and a tin cup pressed to his lips.

"Slow," the man told him. "Just a sip. You'll give yourself cramps otherwise."

There wasn't a brandy in the world that tasted as good as this water, and he followed instructions until he was able to sit up without his stomach charging for his mouth. Then he filled his palms and splashed the liquid over his head and neck.

"I was going to say thanks."

Wolf hunkered down in front of him, the shotgun across his thighs. "No need. You had trouble."

Lincoln blinked away the fuzziness of his vision and saw that his first impression was correct—the stranger was an Indian.

"How'd you find me?"

Wolf pointed to a dusty motorcycle parked a hundred yards away, alongside the arroyo. "I heard the snakes, saw you playing Tarzan, and figured you for a tourist. They do that, you know. They park by the road, take a few steps off, and get totally lost. Happens all the time. They watch too many westerns."

He grinned, and accepted another drink. "I wasn't exactly strolling. There was an accident."

"Big old Caddy?"

"Right." But caution kept the humor from his smile. "Me and my girl."

"Oh, you're Annabelle's guy?"

"You know her?"

"You could say that," he said with a smile. "I'm her mother's widower. She may have spoken of me. Annabelle, that is. Her mother isn't saying much of anything these days."

Linc lifted a hand for a moment's silence, lowered his head, and stared at his boots. This was Annabelle Bannon's stepfather, he'd been told of the accident, knew the woman must be hurt, and hadn't yet asked what had happened.

"What happened?"

Serves you right, he thought glumly. "Somebody ran us off the road."

"You all right?"

"Now I am, yes, but don't you think we ought to go back and see about Annabelle?"

Wolf shook his head, and took a drink from the canteen.

"Why the hell not?"

"Because I'm not there."

He did not move, and did not act surprised when she stepped out from behind a shrub and crouched down beside her stepfather. The resemblance was uncanny, more so when he flashed an image of Loraleen on the other side. And he knew he was staring when she laughed and nudged Wolf's side.

"He sees."

"He's not blind," said Wolf without looking away.

"No one else does."

"Sees what?" Lincoln asked.

"What you see," Wolf told him.

He scratched at his brow and behind one ear. "I think I must still be groggy. I don't get it."

"Another time," Wolf told Annabelle when she started to explain.

She shrugged, then moved beside Lincoln to examine his injuries. On her own forehead was a large ugly bruise raised on a fleshy mesa. Every so often she would narrow her eyes against the sporadic pain, but except for that and some light scratches on the backs of her hands, she seemed fit enough. She nodded when he asked her silently, then told him she'd come to five or ten minutes after the crash, lying on the side of the road. She'd searched for him for nearly an hour, staying close to the highway and hoping she'd be able to get a ride to the ranch, or back to the nearest town. Wolf had driven by just as she'd given up and was going to walk.

"Our friend didn't come back?" he said, astonished.

"Nope. When I came around, he was gone and so was the truck."

"Great. I mean, that's good for you, bad for us. It means he's still out here."

"Who?" Wolf asked. "Or is it a secret?"

Without detailing the reasons for his visit, Linc described the man in black and what he'd done. The Indian's expression didn't change, but the grip on his weapon tightened perceptibly.

"I just wish I knew who he was," he finished. "He has a twin I'd like to introduce to those snakes over there."

"They already know him."

Annabelle frowned; Linc rose slowly, gripping the small of his back and stretching without taking his gaze from the man's face. "How so?" he said.

"Peter," said Annabelle, "do you know this guy?"

Wolf hesitated before nodding.

Lincoln waited.

"Well?" she prompted.

"The white one is Rain," he said quietly, "and the dark one is Storm."

Wonderful, Linc thought; I've been clobbered halfway across the country by a couple of walking skeletons and this idiot gives me a dose of Indian mythology.

"Peter," Annabelle scolded as she got to her feet and stood over him. "C'mon, stop fooling around." She looked nervously out over the desert. "What're their names?"

Wolf gathered up the cup and canteen, and stuffed them in a small leather pouch fixed to his belt. He stood, looked from one to the other, and Linc realized he was much older than he appeared. Much older. There was grey streaked through his hair, and the lines about his mouth and eyes were more distinct as his expression changed.

"Storm and Rain," he said finally, "are their names, their real names. Their last name is Manto."

"Oh," said Lincoln, "hell."

"What?" Annabelle said when she saw him rub a hand hard down his chest.

"Manto," he said. "Tremain Manto."

"You know them?"

"We've met."

Once or twice, he thought, and once was enough. The last he had heard of Tremain Manto and his kin, they were up in Canada, living so deep in the north woods that not even the Mounties bothered to hunt them. When he and the Mantos had last crossed paths, Lincoln had been forced to kill an aunt, cripple an uncle, and in the course of his escape toss a pot of quicklime into Tremain's face.

And that was after they had . . .

He sniffed, shook his head violently, and suggested they head for the Bannon ranch so he could be alone, safely, to think.

Without asking questions, Wolf agreed, and with much silent jockeying they all managed to fit onto the motorcycle. A kick start filled the desert with unaccustomed sound, and Lincoln, sitting in back with his arms around Annabelle's waist, could not stop looking at every tree, every cactus, every boulder larger than a gnat. This, he thought, was too damned easy. He had never known a Manto to leave his or her victim so many chances to live . . . unless Storm was simply enjoying himself, as his brother might have been.

Or unless they were simply waiting for something to happen, something he didn't know about that perhaps Annabelle or Peter did.

They headed deeper into the desert, directly toward the towering range rising darkly ahead of them. The clouds were still there, and when he wasn't biting his lips at the lumps his buttocks were taking, he was watching the lightning strikes on the peaks and listening to the thunder.

He was sure, however, that he heard the gunshot just before the front tire blew and the bike slipped slowly, inexorably, over the bank of the arroyo. He was the first to throw himself to one side, Annabelle second, but Peter was caught between the sliding vehicle and the ground. When they reached him, he was unconscious, and his right pants leg was stained with fresh blood.

"Not broken," she said, kneeling over him. "But damn!"

"But you know the way, right?" he said, uneasy at how loud the thunder was growing.

"Sure, but it's still a couple of miles, and I don't know how really serious this is."

"Look," he said, "you go ahead, I'll stay with Peter, and—"

The thunder sounded like a herd of stampeding bison, and he looked to the far end of the arroyo just as a jack rabbit leapt out of the riverbed and raced away.

"Okay," he said, abruptly nervous, thinking about the earthquakes she'd mentioned in the car. "First thing is, we get him out of here."

It didn't take them long to find enough wood and brush to rig a makeshift stretcher, and less time to locate a worn slant of ground they could take him up without much jarring. Then Lincoln slid back down to fetch the shotgun.

He leaned over the bike, found what he wanted, and looked up. Just as a flash flood roared around the bend.

TEN

The water exploded against the wall of the sharp outside bend, thick spray rising up and over the banks, uprooting plants, gushing in and out of burrows and rock holes. It wasn't deep, no higher than Lincoln's waist, but its power was evident by the boulders and saplings it carried effortlessly with it; it wasn't clear and sparkling, it was muddy and foaming and streaked through with writhing bands of black, of yellow, of an unpleasantly faint red that looked too much like blood; and it wasn't silent—its thunder came from collisions with the banks, and its lightning was a loud and steady hissing that sounded too much like the snakes he'd just escaped.

He dropped the shotgun and leapt for the incline, slipped back and scrambled again, just as the water punched his legs and drove him onto his side. He looked up helplessly and saw Annabelle standing at the lip, watching him grimly with hands on her hips, watching his fingers dig uselessly into the ground as the suction beneath the surface began dragging him down, twigs and branches gouging into his shins, rocks pummeling his thighs. He reached out a hand as the water slipped along his back and pulled him lower, his fingers extended, his eyes wide and waiting without bothering to beg.

She wanted him dead, and the way she was studying him, he thought in the brief moment before the first wave crashed over his head, she was trying to decide if this could look like an accident, or if there'd be some sort of trouble with the authorities later.

Then the water took him, and he barely managed a deep breath before he was taken under, rolled and tumbled, with one hand still trying to break the surface while the other attempted to protect his head from splitting against the bottom, the banks, against the dark forms he saw being pushed past him.

He knew he had little time; once the flood reached the next bend, he would be smashed to less than a pulp, and not even the fabled Knight's powers would be able to put him back together again.

Then something snared his wrist.

The water's rush increased, and he swallowed mud and grime as he tried to free himself. Instead of being crushed now, he was going to drown.

The tugging increased, and without quite understanding why, he managed to get his feet against the riverbed and shove upward. His head broke into the air, and he gasped, sputtered, and clawed for the bank. Someone was holding him. Annabelle, and he thought nothing of it until his feet found purchase and, with her help, he had fallen over the embankment onto dry ground.

He choked. He gagged. He rolled onto his stomach, held himself up and retched until his stomach was empty.

He looked up at the woman kneeling in front of him.

"Thanks," he whispered.

She shrugged.

"No, really, thanks."

"It's okay," she said. "I had a little attack of conscience, I guess."

He allowed her the attack, and said, "You do that again and I'll kill you."

Her expression wavered between a smile and something akin to fear, decided on the smile, and helped him to his feet. He made her wait for a moment until he was sure his legs were working again, and waited a moment longer while the pounding in his head faded to a dull ache. Then they staggered together back to where Peter Wolf was still lying unconscious, and when he looked down at his clothes, he realized he was already virtually dry. Only a gritty feeling on his hands and face remained, and a few moist blades of grass clinging to his hair. He nodded, and walked back to the arroyo, looked down and shook his head—there was little left of the flood now save a few ribbons of dark water meandering along the center of the riverbed. He guessed that by nightfall there wouldn't be a drop left.

Neither the shotgun nor the motorcycle were anywhere to be seen.

Annabelle stood just behind him, and he tensed, waiting, until she said, "Now what?"

"Now we walk," he said. "And I hope you have a bathtub that isn't rigged to electrocute me."

"Now listen," she said. "About—"

"Later!" he snapped. And as he walked back to her stepfather, he said over his shoulder, "And I wasn't kidding before."

He thought his hand would cramp permanently after the first mile of carrying the ill-made stretcher; he thought his arms would fall off after he lost track of time. Annabelle, on the other hand, seemed not to be bothered, and the only reason he didn't demand a halt for recuperation was so not to give her the satisfaction of seeing him drop.

Dumb, he thought; and still he kept on.

It was an hour after dark when they finally reached the barbed-wire fence that surrounded what he estimated was three or four acres of incredibly lush grass. Small yellow globes attached at regular intervals on fenceposts cast shadows on the lawn, and sprinklers filled the air with an odd rainbow mist. Once through the wooden gate they lowered Wolf to the ground and waited to catch their breath.

The house was at the base of a low hill, and as far as he could tell, it sprawled in a hundred different directions at once, additions made by whim rather than necessity. The porch was covered by an open-beamed roof, the windows were slightly rounded, and the walls made of adobe.

"Nice place," he said, bending down to take the foot of the makeshift stretcher.

"Yeah," she said thoughtfully, and they started for the door.

From somewhere in back a dog began to bark.

"Awfully quiet out here."

"Yeah."

And when she reached the porch, she stopped, cocked her head, and listened.

"Expecting somebody?"

She nodded. "We have five people working here at the house. They should have seen us by now."

He spat and licked his lips, nodded for her to open the door and get them inside. At the moment he wasn't concerned about the state of her hired help; right now his bones and every muscle in his body were aching, and all he wanted to do was get Wolf into a bed, fix up his leg, and find his own first aid before he literally fell apart.

Once inside, however, he wasn't so sure he wasn't in the middle of an interior decorator's nightmare.

The foyer itself was unassuming, tiled in dark grey, and the walls beamed with dark-stained wood. To their left, however, was the living room, and he couldn't help it—he had to lower his end of the stretcher again. Annabelle took it as a signal to find someone to help them, and she hurried on down a dark narrow hall. Linc just stood there, hands on his hips.

The room was easily thirty feet on a side, with massive, walk-in stone fireplaces in two walls, and more furniture on braided and oriental carpets than he'd seen in the last warehouse he was in. The walls were covered with expensive, handmade Navajo rugs interspaced with gold-framed velvet paintings of bullfighters, naked women, and prowling panthers; three wagon wheel chandeliers hung from the high ceiling over the three areas of the room where the furniture was most concentrated; over each fireplace were mounted collections of Spanish swords, Indian bows, and what looked to him like plastic flintlocks, while on the mantelpieces themselves were dozens of cheaply framed photographs of Annabelle, Loraleen, Peter, and a woman he assumed was Maybelle Bannon Wolf. There were audio speakers in each corner, and they were playing Mantovani.

Astonishing, he thought. Absolutely astonishing.

A low groan, then, from behind him, and he turned to look at Wolf. The Indian was struggling to sit up, his wide glazed eyes blinking rapidly while one hand grabbed tentatively for his injured leg.

"Take it easy," Linc said, kneeling beside him. A quick examination found no fresh blood, and without asking permission he grabbed a knife from the man's belt and began cutting open his trouser leg. He hissed when he pulled the material apart.

"How bad is it?" Wolf asked, his voice drugged with pain.

From the middle of the thigh to the middle of the shin, the skin was badly scraped, the flesh raw and still oozing dark welts of blood around the bend of the knee.

Wolf winced when he saw it. "Beautiful. Just beautiful. Where's Annabelle?"

Lincoln peered down the hall. "She went for help. Seems your people are never around when you need them."

Wolf pushed himself higher, gritted his teeth, and looked over his shoulder. "I don't like it," he said calmly. "Not the leg, the house. The leg isn't as bad as it looks. I think the house is. If you go straight on back there, you'll end up in the kitchen. Go on," he ordered. "I'll be okay here."

Lincoln hesitated, then put the knife into Wolf's hand and hurried away, reached the kitchen, and pushed the door inward. The overhead lights were fluorescent and on, too bright for him to see clearly at first. He waited until his vision adjusted, and wondered if they regularly fed an army from here. Three stoves, three refrigerators, two stand-up freezers, and cabinets, hanging utensils, and four island counters set in a row to the back door.

He was going to call out, but changed his mind when he heard the silence. A silence too deep for his instincts to ignore. On the balls of his feet, then, he moved to his right and passed down the aisle between the counters and the ovens. He could hear nothing but the refrigerators, and as he passed each counter, he paused and leaned over to stare at the white floor.

Between the third and fourth ones he found Annabelle.

She was lying on her side, one arm under her head, and after a quick check to be sure she was merely unconscious, he went to the back door, stood to one side, and switched off the lights. The room instantly became black, with only a few red eyes from the ceiling smoke alarms to break the monotony. The door opened silently. He stepped out and to one side, dropping immediately into a crouch and scanning the rear yard.

It was only half again as large as the front, since the hill began immediately on the other side of the fence. There were no lights here, the only illumination from the stars and a huge pale moon lifting over the mountains. The back walls of the house were clear, and there was nothing he could interpret as the sound of someone moving furtively across the grass.

A moan, and he was back inside, kneeling by Annabelle and helping her sit up.

"I don't think I like playing with you, Blackthorne," she said, gingerly rubbing the back of her head.

"Did you see him?"

"No." She grabbed the edge of the counter and pulled herself up. "I heard him, or one of them, and came back here to look. The next thing I knew, there were stars." She smiled wanly. "You really do see stars, you know that? Boy, and here I thought that stuff was all fake."

With a hand at her waist he helped her back to the foyer. Wolf had somehow maneuvered himself against the wall so he could see the door and the hallway without turning his head. He smiled when he saw his stepdaughter, and shrugged to Lincoln when she gasped at the sight of his injured leg. Before she could break down, he told her to get him some damp cloth and something he could use for a bandage, and a crutch.

"You're not going anywhere," Lincoln told him after the woman had gone.

"Well, if you think I'm going to sit here all night, you're crazy."

"Give me a number and I'll call a doctor. That leg needs attention, and soon."

Wolf raked his hands through his hair, looked up, and shook his head. "There's no time, Mr. Blackthorne. Those men are around here somewhere, and they aren't going to wait until I'm patched up before they make their next move."

"Which is?"

Wolf spread his hands.

"Well, damnit!" He stalked into the living room, glared at the clutter, and turned around. "None of this makes sense, you know. None of it. I had assumed, you see, that Annabelle knew—" He stopped, frustrated, more so when he saw the slight smile on the Indian's face.

"It's all right, Mr. Blackthorne," the man said. "I know why you're here. Annabelle told me."

"She did?"

"She had to."

"She did?"

"Of course."

He looked to his left, at a gleaming Castilian saber over the fireplace, and wondered if he had it in him to fetch it, put it against Wolf's throat, and run him through if he didn't stop talking in riddles. When he looked back, Annabelle had returned and was, amid a great number of protests from both herself and her stepfather, washing the grit and dried blood away as best she could. He stepped heavily to the doorway with his hands on his hips, waiting none too patiently for her to finish.

It took a long time, and neither of them were inclined to pay him much attention.

He tapped his foot, shifted his weight, and finally checked and rechecked the doors to be sure they were locked. He checked the rest of the house. He checked it twice. When he returned from his second tour, he found Wolf propped up on one of the leather sofas, his leg on a brass coffee table and a beer in his hand. He was also wearing a clean pair of trousers.

"Now," he said, "suppose you tell me why Annabelle had to tell you why I came out here."

"You're looking for a horse, right?" Wolf said.

"Not exactly a whole horse," he admitted, scanning the room for Annabelle.

"The tail, then. Of the Arabian, Knight."

"Why am I not surprised you know about it?"

"Because you know that I know where it is."

Lincoln nodded noncommittally. The fact is, he had assumed Annabelle knew where this talisman was; or, in view of her attitude, knew where her uncle at least thought it was.

He was about to ask Wolf a question then when he heard a scuffling at the back of the room. He looked up, startled, and saw Storm Manto wrestling Annabelle across the fireplace hearth. Beside them was Rain, who had snatched down the saber and was grinning as he fingered the edge of the blade.

"Good evening, Mr. Blackthorne," the White Rider said, and before Lincoln could answer, Manto threw the saber directly at his head.

ELEVEN

Annabelle screamed.

Lincoln shoved Peter hard to one side and ducked into a run around the sofa as the saber hummed past his ear and stuck quivering into the wall. His reaction was such that he was across the room before either of the Mantos could think. He butted the White Rider into the mouth of the huge fireplace and gave him no time to recover—his fist struck Rain's temple and he scrambled out again, kicking the logs over his prone form. Then he whirled to face Storm, who held a bowie knife to Annabelle's throat and was smiling.

"Nice try, Mr. Blackthorne."

Lincoln's fists hung loosely at his sides, but for the moment he could see no way to attack and get past the cutting of the woman's throat. A shrug, then, and a grim wondering what had happened to the house's missing staff. He decided it probably wasn't polite to ask.

Rain struggled grumbling out of the fireplace, clamped his hat back onto his straggly, deadwhite hair, and dusted angrily at his clothes, now more pocked grey than white. He growled, and pulled a revolver from his waistband, thumbed the hammer back, and jammed the barrel into Lincoln's spine. He would have pulled the trigger right then had not Storm grunted an order. Rain glowered, and Lincoln prayed the other Manto was still the stronger.

He was. After another sharp jab to be sure Lincoln remembered the gun, Rain eased the hammer back into position and gestured with the weapon impatiently until Lincoln and the woman were sitting on the couch, Peter Wolf between them. Storm made sure they weren't going to try anything, then closed the drapes on the windows; Rain pushed back the coffee table and sat on it, examining the gun lovingly and humming.

"I suppose," Lincoln said calmly, "we're all here for the same thing."

"You got it, Blackthorne," Storm said with a slightly distasteful look at his brother.

"I can tell you two right now I won't tell you where it is," Wolf said angrily.

"I think you will."

Wolf was about to respond when Lincoln jabbed him with an elbow that made him grunt. The signal was clear—they were in no position to bargain. For the time being, the Mantos were in charge. Rain gave them all his death's-head smile.

"Now," said Storm, standing just behind his brother with his hands loose on his hips, "you gonna make it easy, or is my brother here gonna have to play games?"

Wolf shook his head stubbornly.

"Not a good choice," Manto said, clucking.

And as Lincoln groaned silently, Rain casually swung the barrel around until it was aimed at the middle of Annabelle's forehead.

"Are you sure?"

"Don't say a word, Peter," Annabelle said bravely. "They're bluffing."

"Now wait a minute," Lincoln protested.

But Rain pulled the trigger, Annabelle whimpered and squeezed her eyes shut, and the click of the hammer falling on an empty chamber made Lincoln half rise from his seat.

"One bullet," Storm said when Annabelle stopped flinching and Linc found a way to start his lungs working again. "My brother is crazy—he likes Russian roulette. Like I said, one bullet. I don't know where it is. Do you know where the tail is?"

Wolf folded his arms defiantly over his chest.

Rain pulled the trigger again.

Annabelle changed her mind about bravado and huddled deep in the corner, pleading silently.

A third time, and Lincoln wondered how long his nerves would hold out, how long it would be before he lunged at the White Rider and was rewarded for his heroism with a knife in his chest. He looked at Wolf, who had aged considerably, the lines in his face now more like the arroyos he'd seen in the desert.

Rain pulled the trigger a fourth time, and Annabelle sat up abruptly and slapped her stepfather's arm. "Hey, damnit!" she said.

Wolf looked at them both, then at the Mantos, and sagged. "All right, all right."

Rain seemed disappointed, but rose from the table and filled the empty chambers quickly with cartridges from his belt. Storm took his place, fingering the knife and smiling.

"Well?" he said.

"Konochine Pueblo," the Indian muttered.

Rain frowned. "Where the hell is that?"

"I'll give you directions. It's easy when you know how to get there."

"Don't sound right to me," the White Rider complained.

Storm, however, nodded once. "Fair enough," he said briskly while Rain began pacing the length of the room, mumbling the name over and over again and shaking his head.

Lincoln relaxed, but only slightly. There was something not quite right about the scene, but he couldn't pin it down. Instead of fretting then, he kept his eye on Rain, whose agitation was growing, and growing dangerously. Storm seemed oblivious to it, but he knew it wouldn't be long before the two of them decided that there was no sense keeping any of them alive once the route was mapped out. They may be a bit slow, he thought, but they weren't completely stupid.

To stall until he could think things through, and perhaps be the grateful recipient of a minor but spectacular miracle, he asked Peter how the Arabian magician's talisman came to be in a place like that. Wolf looked at him puzzledly, but when Lincoln asked him again and even the Mantos seemed interested, he explained that the Spanish during their conquests of the Southwest had been notorious for their unflagging and almost fanatical attempts to convert the Indians to Christianity.

Sometimes it worked, and there was little trouble from the local population.

There were other times, however, when the Indians decided

they'd had enough of what often amounted to religious slavery, and they revolted, driving the Spanish from the land in a series of bloody and very unchristian battles. During one of these uprisings a Spanish priest, who was no fool despite his piety and who had been using the healing artifact as an incentive to Christian conviction, hid in the pueblo to avoid being killed.

That didn't work at all.

He was found, tortured, then thrown into a narrow canyon where, legend had it, the Indians waited for three days to see how he would make himself well. Without the tail, the priest couldn't. Subsequently, in honor of their own bravery and success, the Indians threw a four-day-long party, after which they evidently abandoned Konochine on the assumption that the Spaniards might return some day, less hospitable than before. What they apparently didn't understand was that the power came not from the priest but from the curious gold-braided tail he carried with him in a chest. And when, some years later, the rebellion ultimately failed and the Spanish did in fact return, no one believed the tribe when they told the priest's story, and none of them knew where the chest had been buried.

"Then how do you know?" Storm asked, interested in spite of himself.

"They were my ancestors," Wolf told him sourly. "I didn't believe it either until," he said with a look to Annabelle, "your uncle called with all those reports he had about the tail and how it got over here. And when I remembered the stories, I decided to find out for myself. It took a long time because Konochine's been deserted for centuries, all roads gone, hardly any traces even in the writings, but I found it and snooped around a little. And by damn, there it was."

"Why didn't you bring it back?"

Wolf's gaze shifted to Lincoln. "Do you know where Konochine is?"

"Peter," he said, "I didn't even know where New Mexico was until three days ago."

"If you knew where it was," Wolf said, "you'd know why I didn't bring it back."

"Until now," Storm said, rising.

The Indian shrugged.

Storm grunted something then and his brother joined him, and they conferred just far enough away so that Lincoln couldn't hear them. He scowled, shook his head when Wolf asked if he thought they were going to be freed, then pushed himself to the edge of his seat when the Mantos returned, still keeping the coffee table between them and their prisoners.

Storm slipped the knife into his belt; Rain dusted the revolver's barrel on his sleeve and pointed it at Wolf. "You're coming with us, Tonto," he said.

"What?" Annabelle grabbed her stepfather's arm. "What are you talking about? He can't!"

"Sure he can, if he don't want to die just yet."

"Lincoln!"

"Makes sense to me," Lincoln said, keeping his gaze from the enraged look on her face. "If Peter just gives them directions, how are they going to know he won't just send them on a wild goose chase, thus leaving us free to get the tail ourselves?" He smiled innocently. "Right?"

Storm frowned at him distrustfully. "Right."

"Lincoln, for god's sake," Annabelle said, squirming as if hunting for the courage to jump him.

"And of course, you can't leave the woman here because you need someone to tend Peter's leg if it gets bad again. And you can't leave me here because you need someone to carry Wolf, do the digging, lug the water, and stuff like that because you'll be too busy guarding us. Right?"

Storm's frown deepened. "Right. I think."

"Lincoln, will you please shut up!"

Lincoln ignored her, but prayed she'd be angry enough to forget the Mantos and do something stupid. She did. She finally got up and moved as if to leap over her stepfather to get at his throat. Wolf, on the other hand, caught Linc's quick glance and, when Annabelle was in front of them, kicked out against the table. It struck both men just below the knee, startling them enough to allow Lincoln to launch himself from the couch, angling to grab Rain's arm and thrust the gun upward just as it fired.

There were shouts then, confusion, but Linc concentrated on driving the White Rider back into the wall where his head struck the plaster, stunning him momentarily. A blow to his stomach, another to the side of his face, and the gun was in his hand. He whirled, and Storm was on him, lashing out with a boot to kick the weapon free and send it flying across the room.

The bowie knife glinted once.

Linc backed off while Annabelle rushed to find the Colt, pursued by a revived, staggering Rain, whose vision was still somewhat blurred.

"Dumb," Manto said, waving the knife in front of him. "Very dumb, Blackthorne."

Linc backed to the nearest fireplace, spun and leapt, and came down with a sword. Manto's eyes widened slightly, then feinted just enough to push Lincoln off the hearth. Within moments the bowie had been replaced by a saber.

"Dumb," he said a third time, and lashed out with the blade.

Linc parried, knowing there was no time for finesse, and the room was filled with the clash of steel against steel, sparks winking, the men's boots harsh on the bare flooring. Another parry, and he thrust; Manto jumped back, swung wildly and drove Lincoln to balance on a chair, one foot on the cushion, the other on the back. Manto lunged, Linc slashed and leapt over the back, turned and raised his saber just as Storm closed in on him. Their arms went up, the blades slid along each other with a shrieking, rasping sound, and the rounded hilts locked when they were virtually nose to nose.

He could see the eyes then—lifeless, deep, as if he were looking into a waterless well.

Manto chuckled.

Their arms strained, their feet sought purchase on the slippery floorboards, and perspiration spilled into their eyes.

Lincoln stepped back to bring the man forward, then snapped his wrist to free the lock and leapt to one side. Manto, off balance, stumbled forward, but Lincoln's wild slash at his back missed and he was around again and driving.

Annabelle called out, telling him to be careful. She had Rain backed against a wall, the revolver in her hand.

Wolf was still on the sofa, rubbing his leg lightly and finishing his beer.

They circled the room once, slapping furniture in each other's way, kicking up rugs, Manto once grabbing a lamp and tossing it at Lincoln's head. He ducked, and ducked again as the blade hissed over his scalp, swung his own saber forward and made Storm leap over it. A swing from Linc's blade cleared the mantelpiece of the family photographs; Manto's next thrust sliced through the material on his shirt, just above the elbow. Manto grabbed a log from the andirons, and Lincoln's blow splintered it; Linc feinted a hack at the man's head, lowered his lunge and scratched the silver buckle on Manto's belt.

Then they were circling the room a second time, Lincoln hoping Annabelle would think of something, and soon, because he'd just run out of Douglas Fairbanks movies.

Manto thought of something first; as they passed the fireplace, he grabbed a second blade.

"Well, damn," Linc said.

Manto chuckled, and from behind him he could hear Annabelle's yelp—Rain had managed to take the gun from her.

"Well, damn," he said again, realizing that Storm's brother wasn't going to stop the fight.

He backed warily across the middle of the room, Manto weaving death patterns in the air with his sabers. The only sound was that of their breathing, and the hissing of the steel like serpents seeking his throat. He moistened his lips. Storm kept advancing. He tried to sidestep to the foyer, but Manto blocked him and kept him moving. Backward. Until he was nearing the corner where Annabelle held Rain.

Suddenly, Wolf shouted a warning.

Lincoln took just enough time to glance over his shoulder, just long enough to see Annabelle with her hands raised.

And in them a lamp she brought down on his head.

TWELVE

The airliner was obviously attempting to fly without wings, without an experienced and compassionate pilot, and with only a single engine that coughed and sputtered more than it ran smoothly. It pitched, rolled, dropped, and steadied, jounced abruptly a few times for good measure in order to test the muscles keeping his head from leaving his neck. They weren't doing a very good job; he was waiting with arms tensed to catch it when it fell off. Nor were the in-flight air conditioners turned on—he felt as if he were stretched out in an airborne oven, and wouldn't have been surprised if on opening his eyes he found an apple in his mouth.

The problem was, all things considered, he didn't want to open his eyes and look down at the place where he was soon going to crash.

But at least, he thought, for the time being he wasn't dead.

Without much effort he could feel that his arms and legs were still reasonably attached and perhaps even functioning, could feel the dull ache that crawled along his spine, and if he turned his head just so, he could enjoy the throbbing lump that had grown in his hair. He could also feel sound—an engine's roaring that sent sparks dancing on his skin and made him wish he were temporarily deaf.

All in all, it was incredible how the plane managed to stay in the air; all in all, equally incredible that he'd made it back to the airport without getting killed.

Then he remembered Annabelle and the lamp, and his eyes snapped open.

He was looking at the padded inside roof of a vehicle not a car—a second later he realized it was a van with all the back seats taken out for some reason. There were three bulged and rounded slats for windows on the sides, and in spite of their grey tint the sunlight blared through them in a harsh, sullied white. Extra padding in the form of ragged strips of red shag carpeting had been tacked to the sides, and the flooring he could see was carpeted the same; bolted to the side above his head was an empty gun rack, and on the other side was a brace that held the shell of a television set not much bigger than a tin of cookies.

There was the faint smell of gasoline, of trapped heat, of the sweat that had soaked into and dried on his clothes.

He had an abrupt, cold feeling he would have been safer in the wingless plane.

With small, tentative movements, then, trying not to make any noise and alert the keepers of this roving luxury prison, he discovered he was lying awkwardly against the van's left wall, on an uncomfortable bed made of piled rough army blankets that smelled faintly of mothballs; his head was propped on what felt like a canvas knapsack filled with rocks. Slowly, he turned and looked to the left and saw four other knapsacks stacked against the opposite wall. On one side of the pile Peter Wolf was dozing, legs drawn up with his hands cupped around his knees; on the other side was Annabelle— she was wide awake, and staring somewhat doubtfully at him.

He assayed a smile to prove he was real.

She glanced toward the front, took a breath, and glanced back as she brushed a trembling hand back through her hair.

"You're not dead."

"No thanks to you," he said hoarsely.

She handed over a canvas-covered canteen, and he took it after two abortive tries, sipped from it gratefully, and handed it back. The water was warm, but it tasted awfully damned good. A moment more, and he rolled onto his side, groaned, and sat up.

"I had to do it," she explained before he could ask the obvious question.

A finger gingerly probed the circumference of the lump. "Sure you did."

"If I hadn't, he would have killed you."

"Why didn't you hit him, then?"

"Then Rain would have killed me."

"Ah." Priorities, he knew, could be a pain sometimes. "So where are we?" He looked out the nearest smoked-glass window, turned away, and looked again.

"Beautiful, isn't it?" she commented dryly.

"Lovely," he muttered, and would have shaken his head had he been sure it would stay on.

There was nothing out there but desert—various species of dust-covered cactus, straggling shrubs that had long since lost their green, gritty sand, and sun-baked rocks that were an unpleasant pale brown. The horizon was ragged with the vague promise of mountains, and the air above them was tinged faintly purple. It didn't take him long to see that they weren't on a highway, a country road, or even a prospector's well-worn trail.

"We're going to Konochine," she said when he asked again. "We've been on the road since dawn."

"I've been out that long?"

She pulled nervously at her short hair. "The guy in black gave you an extra tap when you started to come around. He didn't want you to give him any trouble."

"Wonderful."

"He would have killed me if I tried to stop him."

"I commend your sense of self-preservation."

He looked up front, at the high-backed seats covered with the same red shag. Storm was driving intently, grunting at each slam against the tires, wrestling to keep the steering wheel from jerking out of his hands; Rain, on the other hand, was staring at a sheet of wrinkled paper in his hands, every so often looking up and out and tapping a bony finger against some faintly positioned landmark. A questioning look, and Annabelle told him Peter had drawn them a map to the pueblo, a rough one but fairly serviceable as long as he was with them. And yes, she said, his leg was still sore but working better.

Wolf slept on.

Rain turned around at the sound of voices and grinned at Lincoln, tapped his brother's shoulder, and looked back to the map. Storm turned briefly, gave him a two-fingered salute, and cursed loudly when they plunged briefly into a hidden depression around a tall cactus.

Lincoln groaned at the dull bells suddenly set to ringing in his head, accepted another drink of water and, from a bag by the woman's side, a sandwich wrapped in wax paper. Roast beef, with mustard, a sweet gherkin, and crisp, moist lettuce. On rye. With the crust neatly sliced off.

"Don't tell me," he said when her mouth opened. "If you hadn't made food, they would have killed you."

"Well, they would have."

He shifted awkwardly until he could see between the brothers, squinting, then shading his eyes with one hand against the setting sun. More desert, the oddly placed mesa, the mountains in the distance.

"I don't suppose there's any sense in asking how far we are from civilization."

"No," she said, "because I don't know." She tapped a window lightly with her knuckle. "Once we left the ranch, we headed northeast, then north. I thought we were heading for Portales, but they stopped for a while with the map and changed direction again. When we left the road, I got completely lost." Her smile was sweet and apologetic. "I haven't the faintest idea where we are. We could have traveled in circles for all I know, and Peter isn't doing much talking."

"In other words, if I jump out of here right now in a daring bid for freedom, manage not to get myself caught, and strike out on my own, I'll be dead before morning."

"Before midnight," she said ruefully.

He considered it, looked at the harsh landscape again, and sat back, mimicking Wolf's position and shaking his head. "You know," he said quietly, "I was actually going on a vacation before all this happened. The first real vacation I've had in a number of years. I thought about heading for someplace exotic, and then I decided it would be more fun, and different, to go up to Maine." He wiped a sleeve over his forehead and down over his face, and made a face at the dark stain the perspiration left behind. "It's cool up there. The moose like it a lot. I would too, I think. And you'll forgive me if I say that as beautiful as this desert is, in its own macabre way, I think I'd rather see a tree. In Maine. With a moose."

"I know how you feel."

He wondered if she did. She was supposed to be on his side, yet so far she hadn't exactly proved it to a jury: she had admitted without prompting to sometimes wishing her uncle dead so she could inherit the horse farm and leave this state; she had clonked him with a cupid-shaped lamp in self-defense against somebody else; and she had taken her own sweet time deciding whether or not to pull him out of a flash flood. It was getting awfully hard these days to know who to depend on.

An hour later the mesa didn't seem any closer.

An hour after that the sun dropped abruptly below the horizon. There was no dusk, no lingering twilight, nothing romantic about it at all; one minute there was a flaring of crimson and orange in the western sky, and the next it had all been replaced by a perfectly solid and decidedly unfriendly black. If it hadn't been for the crescent moon and the remarkable number of stars, they might just as well have been in a tunnel.

Annabelle dozed fitfully with her head on her knees, Wolf still hadn't awakened, and except for an occasional warning glance, the Mantos were too busy trying to keep their vehicle from smashing into cacti and dropping into dead rivers that kept cropping up whenever they weren't wanted.

In such preoccupied company Lincoln could do nothing else but prepare a long mental list of exquisite tortures to test on Upshire when he returned, and try to figure out not only why the Mantos were so interested in Knight's tail, but how they had learned about it in the first place. It was a little piece of information Farren had, in his quaint bumpkin way, neglected to pass on.

The van stopped.

Lincoln, feeling much better though stiff around the knees and the back of his neck, tensed when Rain turned on the inside light and looked over the seat. The barrel of the revolver poked up beside his cheek and wriggled until he understood they were being ordered outside. He debated making a move—if he could deflect the gun's aim, the closeness of the interior would give him an advantage in immobilizing the brothers at least temporarily, and with Annabelle's help they might actually get away with it. In fact, they had a good chance of it.

With, he thought again, Annabelle's help.

Oh well, he sighed silently, then turned and faced the back. The doors were stuck, and he had to slam the heels of his hands against them before they'd swing open. Remembering the piñon tree, he made a cautious check for snakes before climbing down, groaning at the needles erupting along his legs, and helped Annabelle down beside him.

The Mantos exited from their doors, whispering to each other as they walked about in the glow of the van's headlamps, stretching their legs, laughing once and slapping each other's shoulder as if they were buddies on a simple fishing trip. They paid no attention to the others; out here they didn't need to.

Wolf slept on.

"Is he dead?" he asked with a jerk of his head.

"No, they gave him something."

"Damn," he muttered, and reached in, grabbed his satchel, and opened it. There, amid the rolled clothes, he found Palmer's case, and examined the vial. It was a quarter empty. It didn't take him long to figure out how they knew—Palmer, ever efficient, had pasted a small label onto the glass, and had written a row of Z's across it. There was also a tiny face drawn underneath, its eyes closed in blissful sleep.

"What are we going to do now?" Annabelle asked him quietly, leaning close and taking hold of his arm. "We'll get there about noon tomorrow, they said. They're going to kill us as soon as they find the chest."

"Yes, I guess so."

"Then why don't we stop them now and go back?"

His grip on her shoulders was light, and in the moonlight he realized that she was much more lovely than he'd thought. Her ebony hair was softer, the planes of her face touched with the shadow of the remarkably bright moon. He was tempted to kiss her, but a sudden warning in her eyes made him smile instead.

"Because," he said, "I still work for your uncle."

"He'll never know."

"I will."

"You're trying to make me feel guilty," she accused, though she said it with a smile.

He would have answered her, but was interrupted by a roar of laughter as the Mantos came around the side of the van. Rain was holding an electric lantern, which gave his already skeletal face an even more morbid cast; Storm was holding both guns, and he leaned back against the rear bumper, reached in, and nudged Wolf's leg. The Indian didn't stir.

"Powerful stuff," Manto said.

Lincoln made no comment.

Rain held the lantern higher, its yellow glow not affecting at all the night's black wall surrounding them. "Just want to be sure you don't get any ideas about making a run for it."

"Wouldn't think of it," Lincoln assured him.

"Fine." Storm sniffed, took off his hat, and wiped his brow. "Then I want you to get some sleep. We got a bad day ahead tomorrow, and I don't want to have to leave you behind."

Lincoln stopped him from leaving with his name. "Why did you bring me in the first place?"

"Oh," the man said, "I just had a hunch we might be needing you, that's all."

"Storm," Rain cautioned.

"Don't worry about it," Manto said angrily. "I can take care of myself."

"Yeah, but—"

A hand lashed out, and Rain jerked away from a stinging slap to his cheek. The lantern wobbled, almost dropped, and lightning seemed to crackle through the tension between them. They faced each other with a glare until Rain said, "The tailor," and Storm sagged as if the air had been punched out of his lungs. He stared at the ground, then nodded, looked up and sideways, and grinned.

"Blackthorne," he said, "I'll give you a hint."

Lincoln waited.

Rain raised a hand as if ready to stop his brother again, then shrugged and dropped it.

"It's all right," Manto said without looking away. "Don't worry. I just want to tell the man that our daddy would like to see him again."

"Oh," Lincoln said. "But I thought I heard someplace that he had had himself an accident."

"Oh, he did, he did," Storm said, straightening with a harsh, barking laugh. "And he's gonna get himself all better, don't you worry about it."

"I'm not," he said flatly.

"Didn't think so. Now if you're ready, Mr. Blackthorne, you and the lady get yourselves back inside. Wouldn't want a stray coyote taking you away for a midnight snack."

"Coyotes?" He looked at Annabelle. "You didn't say anything about coyotes."

"I didn't say anything about anything," she told him, and climbed back into the van without his help.

"Coyotes," he mumbled as the Mantos parted to let him pass. "There sure as hell aren't any coyotes in Maine."

He grabbed onto a door handle to haul himself up, annoyed that even the mention of those scavengers would send shivers up his limbs and make him hear thunder. But he froze with one foot braced against the bumper. The thunder was louder, the shivers continued, and they weren't from the coyotes.

"Annabelle," he said.

Then the van began to rock slowly, something split and crashed to the ground out in the dark, and he just had time to push himself away before the earthquake struck.

THIRTEEN

It wasn't much of a quake. The earth neither opened dark caverns to swallow them all, nor did it split like racing ground-lightning into gullies that crisscrossed the desert floor; but it did roll sharply enough to topple Wolf out of the van, to throw Annabelle helplessly from side to side against the carpeted walls, and it was sufficient to flap the van's doors like ponderous metal gullwings. The righthand one smacked a bellowing Rain full in the face and knocked him off his feet, the lantern spinning from his grip and bouncing wildly until it came up against a rock and shone its wide beam at the stars; the left caught Storm on the shoulder and shoved him back, arms flailing, each of his guns firing once harmlessly into the air.

Lincoln, who had been toppled to his hands and knees while trying to avoid being pinned under a tire, saw Rain fall. He kicked back immediately and launched himself at him, landing just off target because of the quake's pitch and yaw. He was close enough, however, to grab one of the Colts, crawl frantically over the hoarsely swearing man to grab the other, and rock up to his feet without getting caught.

Almost immediately the earthquake subsided.

The only sound it left behind was the creaking of the van as it settled back onto its tires.

They waited, nerves tuned for aftershocks, for the slightest hint that it wasn't quite over.

Somewhere in the distance, a coyote howled.

Linc finally walked over to Storm, who was moaning and clutching at his injured shoulder. He looked down and brought both guns forward. Manto's eyes widened in fear, looking less like a skeleton now than a man facing the end. His fingers twitched on the triggers, but he couldn't bring himself to do it. *Just a tap*, Annabelle had told him the man had delivered to keep him safely unconscious; *just a tap, that's all.* He shrugged, flipped one of the guns to hold it by the barrel and gave Storm the same consideration with the white ivory stock. The man jumped, his legs went rigid, and his eyes opened wide in dismay before he sighed, relaxed, and lay down again.

"Lincoln?"

"Here." He turned as Annabelle unsteadily crawled out of the van, brushing hair from her eyes and looking around, shaken but no longer scared.

"Are you all right?"

She nodded jerkily.

"Great, then go get the lantern."

She obeyed without question, though he could see that her legs were not quite ready yet to do exactly what she wanted. When she returned, they checked on Rain, whose face was bloodied on the right side. He was unconscious, and Linc wasted no time handing the guns over to Annabelle and bending down at the man's feet.

"What . . . Lincoln, for heaven's sake, what are you doing?"

He replied by pulling off each of the man's boots, running a short distance back in the direction they'd come and flinging them into the dark as far as he could, not moving until he heard them thud on the ground. He did the same to Storm, then asked if there was, by any slim chance, some rope available.

There was, the Mantos had brought it, and he soon had the brothers trussed snugly and placed a good fifty yards apart, off the trail they were taking. Then they hoisted Wolf back inside, slammed and locked the doors, and climbed wearily into the front seats.

"Lincoln," she said as he started the engine, "you're not going to leave them out there, are you?"

He thought about that for a minute—the predators of the night searching for their meals, the invisible desert killers that moved only after sunset, the sun itself burning hotly shortly after dawn. There was always the chance of another earthquake, this one more than simply a minor stretching exercise. And he thought about all those ugly rattlesnakes that lived in all those ugly little rattlesnake holes.

"Yep."

She shook her head and looked back at her stepfather. "Will he be out long?"

"According to the man who should know, about twenty-four hours, I should think."

The van shuddered as he shifted the recalcitrant gears, grinding them a little as he sought their place in the desert scheme of things, and whined when he released the parking brake and they started to move.

"Where are we going?"

"We were heading for that mesa, right?"

She nodded.

"Then we're heading for that mesa."

"Then what?"

"Then we will get a decent night's sleep, wake up refreshed and able in the morning, and do what we came to do without the help of our nasty friends back there." He smiled grimly. "And while we're on our way, you can tell me a few things—like your life story, for instance."

What he received was a silence that lasted well over an hour. By that time the mesa had begun to grow and, following the head-lamp's twin spears, he realized it was much higher than he'd esti-mated, and a great deal wider at the base. He automatically checked the odometer, noting how an increasing number of stars were blot-ted out by the imposing formation for each mile they traveled. And after fifteen, he felt as if he were in the shadow of an immense land whale, one that gave him a chill despite the fact that the land's own cold had forced him to turn the heater on.

He lost track of time.

Neither the stars nor the moon seemed to move, and there was no landmark close enough to give him an indication of how rapidly he was moving in relation to the world.

Annabelle still refused to talk. Once, she climbed into the back and shifted Wolf around to a more comfortable position, placing a knapsack pillow under his head and bathing his face with water. He murmured but did not awaken. When she returned, she would not look at him, and he wondered what he'd said this time to set off her temper.

A glance in the rearview mirror, and all he could see was a disturbing red glow when he touched the brakes—the devil winking at him, he thought as they neared their destination.

Twenty miles later, with the van acting as if it were ready to puncture its own tires in a desperate act of vehicular suicide, Annabelle touched his arm.

"We'd better stop."

He did. Then he stuck the lantern out the window to shine it above and beyond the reach of the headlamps.

The mesa loomed above them, not straight out of the earth as he'd thought earlier, but from a long slant of ground covered with thick, low shrubs. Boulders evidently loosened by the quake littered the ground in front of them; a tall cactus lay on its side, and something in shadow burrowed into its watery meat.

He switched off the lantern gladly, turned off the lights, and twisted in his seat to peer back at Peter Wolf.

"We'd better get some sleep," he told her flatly, reaching for one of the blankets. "Like the man said before, we have a bad day tomorrow."

She said nothing.

He wrapped himself as snugly as he could, wormed and wriggled until he was almost comfortable. His eyes closed, his mind began to drift, and he heard her voice, distant and hard:

"You left them out there."

Maybe she'll go away, he prayed, if I don't answer.

"Lincoln, you . . . you left those men out there without any protection."

Oh hell, he thought.

"Yes," he said.

"That's . . . that's murder."

One eye opened. "Annabelle, it may not have occurred to you, but they would have killed us without asking our permission. I'm not used to dying unless I'm ready."

"But . . . but . . ." She looked confusedly from side to side, up to the roof, down at her lap, and finally at him. "But we're the *good* guys."

Well, me anyway, he thought sourly.

"I mean, we're not supposed to be the same as they are."

"As I recall, you tried to do me in a couple of times."

"Oh. Well, that was different."

"So is this," he said, yawning hard to prove he was drifting off, and don't bother him with any more stupid comments. "This is different because in this case we stay alive."

"But they—"

"—are the sons of Tremain Manto, and don't for a moment think that I believe them safely dead. Now go to sleep, please. I have to look at some dead Indians in the morning; a great way to start the day."

Five minutes later she nudged him, and he groaned.

"Now what?"

"If they're not dead like you said, shouldn't we be standing guard or something?"

He struggled to sit up, and an arm poked out from the blanket. He pointed at the windshield. "You see that?"

"I don't see anything."

"Right. And neither will they. Should they wake up before dawn, and should they decide to come after us because they're annoyed, and should they be in any condition to do it in the first place, they will not move until they can see. We can take a few drops in holes with this tank; they can't. They'll break a leg, and they don't want that."

"Oh." He couldn't see her face, but he sensed her sudden smile. "Oh!"

"Yeah," he said. "Now go to sleep, Annabelle. I don't like to beg."

Five minutes later she said, "Wanna mess around?"

He groaned, deliberately loudly. "I thought you didn't like men."

"*You* thought I didn't like men. I like men fine."

"Alive?"

"Of course!"

"Then do me a favor and like me in the morning when I'm not half dead from these wonderful accommodations. Touch me now and I'll tear your arm off."

"Tailors are not gentlemen."

"Annabelle," he said plaintively, "do you know a woman named Carmel, in New Jersey?"

Dawn was a torch someone shoved rudely into his face, and he slapped at it angrily, moaned when every square and rounded inch of his body protested the slightest movement, and yelled when his fumbling out of the blanket pushed open the door and he tumbled out. He was on his feet in a hurry, in a ready-to-fight crouch, checking the ground for snakes, the horizon for signs of the Mantos, and his bones for signs of breakage. Then he heard a high-pitched laugh, looked around and saw Annabelle offering him a canteen and a sandwich.

Behind her stood Peter Wolf.

"Welcome back to the world," he grumbled as he grabbed his breakfast ungraciously.

"Best sleep I ever had," the Indian told him. "You've got to give me the recipe when this is over."

"Yeah." He stretched, working the night from his joints. "I'll do that. In fact, I'll even do better. I'll even— What the hell is *that?*"

He had turned around and was facing the mesa, the biggest single rock he'd ever seen in his life.

"Konochine Pueblo," Wolf said.

Lincoln stared. "But I don't see anything but a rock."

"You can't." The man's arm came over his shoulder. "It's up there, on top."

A quick and depressing estimate put the rim of the mesa some two to three hundred feet above the desert floor. Not all of it was straight up—it began with a slope of nearly forty-five degrees, two hundred yards long. Then the cliffs broke skyward. Much was plain brown rock, here and there grey with a fillip of beige; at other places there were streaks of either dark clay or iron ore, and the occasional monster boulder that jutted out in complete defiance of gravity. The walls were not entirely smooth, either—where the wind had not eroded the dirt to grasslike bedrock, the walls were ribbed, creviced, pocked, and marked with prowlike ledges holding stubborn, spindly bushes.

He tilted his head back.

He could see nothing at all on this side that would get him to the top without flying.

With sandwich in hand, then, he herded the others back into the van and drove completely around the mesa, stopping only when Wolf told him to, on the west side where there was a string of low trees and thicker shrubs running several hundred feet parallel to the mesa.

"Water?" he asked in amazement.

Wolf nodded. "There's a stream over there, comes aboveground there to the left, drops back in again over there where the green stops. Interesting."

Lincoln wasn't looking. He was studying the western face, scowling because it was no different than the rest of it. If anything, it was even more imposing. Then he squinted, leaned back and scratched his head, leaned forward again and shaded the sun from his eyes with a hand.

"Y'know," he said, "if I didn't know better, I'd say there was a road up there."

"Bravo," Wolf said, slapping his shoulder. "Not really a road, though. A path. Rather steep, as you can see, but it gets you there." He pointed again, slightly higher. "The perfect fortress, too. Under the rim you can see three levels of caves. The Konochine lived in there, too. Big things once you're inside, and they had ladders to get from one level to the other, and up to the top. When the enemy came up that path, switchbacking on themselves, the Konochine would climb and pull the ladders up after them. Then they'd drop rocks on them, shoot at them, things like that. Crude, but very effective."

"Yeah," he said. He walked back and forth then for several minutes. The climb was going to be steep, and treacherous, and he didn't have to use any imagination at all to picture what those trees back there would look like when they were only halfway up. With no steps, no railings. He didn't think his mother had raised him to be a mountain goat.

Annabelle was unloading the van and checking the contents of the knapsacks. Wolf, who had been helping her and making suggestions, apparently saw Lincoln's nervousness, came over, and took him by the arm. They walked partway up the slope, along stone steps worn almost to the level of the ground. Then he nodded toward a huge shrub bursting with green so dark it seemed unnatural.

"They didn't always use the path," he said.

"What is it?" he asked glumly. "An elevator?"

Wolf laughed. "In a way, white eyes, in a way. I'll show you that first. Then you can decide which way is up."

They were ready in half an hour, and after Lincoln had taken the van in one more circuit of the mesa to look for the Mantos, they shouldered their packs and started off. By eleven they were at the massive bush, and Wolf, with a grimace, pushed his away around it and vanished.

"Nice trick," Linc said, following Annabelle and wishing he would hurry and wake up from this miserable dream. Twigs stabbed at his arms and face, the knapsack kept sliding to one side and throwing him off balance, and the ground was smooth with bedrock and small pebbles that prevented him from gaining any sort of comforting foothold.

Once around the bush, however, he saw the entrance to a cave, and with a silent nod to the extinct tribe, he ducked inside.

The room was small, large enough only for the three of them, and made smaller by the shadows the lantern threw writhing on the wall. Wolf was standing in the center, and when Lincoln finally shoved his way in, cursing and muttering, he stood aside.

"You're kidding," Lincoln said. "You've got to be kidding."

FOURTEEN

Wolf and Annabelle moved aside as Lincoln stepped forward, shaking his head in disbelief. It was insane, of course, some sort of not very funny practical joke being played on the eastern dude. But neither of them were smiling, and he grunted when Wolf lifted the lantern and let the beam trail upward.

It followed the course of an unhealthy-looking rope ladder, handwoven and dangling from the cave's natural chimney in the center of the roof. When he stood next to it and looked up, he could see several hundred feet up a circle of brilliant blue about the size of a saucer. A very small saucer. The kind of saucer you find in a little girl's tea set. He touched the rope and closed one eye; it was rough, and the rungs were braided of the same coarse fiber. It did not appear to be as old as he'd feared, but even if it had been made in the last five minutes, he couldn't believe Wolf was implying they use it. He circled it slowly, head back, finally checking the rungs again.

"Two hundred and eighty-nine," Wolf said quietly, though his voice was loud in the confines of the cave. "One foot apart."

"This is the alternative?" His hands went to his hips. "This is better than the outside?"

"On the outside," the Indian said patiently, "the Mantos can see you and pick you off with a rifle if they're any kind of a shot. Or you could slip on loose soil and kill yourself on the rocks. The wind near the top is freakish and strong; you could be blown off before you knew it. You could freeze if you look down, and we'd be stuck there forever."

He pointed. "You mean I can't fall off *this* thing? You mean I can't freeze in *here?*" He shook his head. "C'mon, Peter, this is madness."

"It works. It's the way I got up." Wolf knelt on the floor and held the bottom rung to keep the rope from swaying. "And the chest is up there."

Annabelle clasped her hands until her knuckles bled white, but offered no argument one way or the other. The sideglow from the lantern gave her face more shadow than he would have liked, and its beam disappeared before it reached the halfway point in the chimney—that he didn't like at all.

"You've come this far," Wolf said.

"I suppose."

"What have you got to lose?"

At first, second, and third inspiration he could think of at least three or four dozen items, none of which would impress the man in the least. So he sighed, dried his hands on his shirt, tightened the knapsack's straps, and, before he could talk himself out of it, took the first step up. The ladder swayed slightly, creaking. He scowled, and waited until Annabelle had joined in the ladder's anchoring. Then he took a deep breath, prayed for no slippery perspiration, and climbed. Slowly. Steadily. Noting that as he entered the chimney the rock walls were much closer together than they appeared from the floor.

"When you get up there—" Annabelle called, her voice small and filled with echoes.

"Yeah?" he said, not stopping.

"—watch out for scorpions."

He stopped.

"Did you hear me?"

"You didn't tell me about the scorpions, Annabelle," he said, not caring about the complaining tone in his voice. "You didn't say anything about scorpions."

"I forgot."

Oh, wonderful, he thought disgustedly, inhaled slowly and started again, trying to pace himself, trying not to swing his weight too far to either side. It wasn't going to be all that bad, he told himself sternly, and every few yards he checked above him, wishing that the saucer would at least have the decency to grow into a platter.

Someone called a question from below, but the words were jumbled and he didn't bother to answer. Instead, he concentrated on not feeling the start of a faint burning on his palms, on not feeling the strain that was beginning to pull at his shoulders and upper arms. His feet thus far were finding the rungs with ease, and as long as he didn't miss, he figured he would be all right.

The air grew cooler.

He could hear water dripping somewhere, and when he peered hard at the nearest section of wall, he realized that the chimney was pocked with small holes, some of them shallow, some rather deep, and none which would provide him with adequate hand- or footholds should he need them.

A strand of spiderweb brushed across his face and without thinking he swiped at it, and suddenly his left foot was reaching for air. He swung slowly in a circle, felt the ladder catch, and he swung back. His foot found purchase. His hands were wet, and his face felt as if he were standing in a shower.

Something else, he ordered; think of something else. Make it mechanical or you're going to fall.

Within seconds he did, especially when he saw what looked like a pair of tiny red eyes staring at him from the wall, and what he thought over the next few minutes he didn't like one bit, not even when he proved that he couldn't be wrong. Unfortunately, there was nothing he could do about it until he reached the top.

He looked down and saw nothing but black.

Above him he could hear the wind soughing across the chimney mouth, and spatters of dust fell on his head and shoulders; the rope creaked and swayed, and by the time he thought of counting his steps, his arms were already threatening to give out. The pain in his shoulders blossomed, and stubbles of fiber from the rungs bit into his fingers, into his palm, and he felt as if he were crawling on sandpaper.

The lantern's beam was gone, and he froze. Though he could see blue overhead, he was in a space of absolute black, and though his thighs and arms protested, he was forced to slow down. One miss, and he would be too exhausted even to think about trying to catch himself.

Another spiderweb. Something light landed on his back and he felt it moving from shoulder blade to shoulder blade; it felt like a giant tarantula, or a giant black widow, or a giant brown recluse, and he arched his back until it scraped in a panic against the cold stone wall. The water, dripping steadily, more loudly now. Something scuttling in one of the larger holes; it sounded like a monster crab's pincers scraping against a sea wall.

He hooked one arm around a rung, wrapped as much of the ladder as he could around one ankle and hung there, swinging from side to side, his mouth and throat dry and rough, his eyes burning, and his head ready to burst.

Up, he said silently; up, you jackass, before you fall asleep.

Shaking his head vigorously, he repositioned his hands and suddenly smiled. He could see them, clearly, and when he looked up, he could see detail around the rim of the mouth. Two dozen steps, and he would make it. Unless, of course, someone cut the moorings.

The thought made him move too fast for prudence, but not fast enough to calm the heart that began to pound in his chest, or stanch the flow of perspiration that crept on spider legs from his hair, ran down his sides and spine, seemed to fill his boots until he was sloshing.

A dozen, and he moved even faster, heedless now of the dangerous tilt of the ladder.

Six, and he was grinning; five, and he was chuckling; the last three taken at such a pace that he didn't even realize that he was abruptly in the open.

Frantically, then, he scrambled until he was lying on his back, gulping the cool air, giggling at the wind that brushed a low cloud of dust over him and matted his hair to his face. Then he rolled over, unslung the knapsack, and took a look around while he waited for the others.

The dwellings of the absent Konochine were in complete ruins. Crumbled adobe walls now less than knee-high in most places were distressing evidence of five large and low buildings that formed a rough circle around what must have been some kind of meeting place for the village—a rectangle of coarse dull grass at least the length of a football field, bordered by what looked like a low tier of three steps, seats perhaps for whatever ceremonies were performed here. Worshiping their gods, weddings, funerals, rites of passage, and the like—he refused to consider the possibility of human sacrifice. Outside the main buildings were others, much smaller, and even more in ruins. The only full-standing wall had a rounded doorway in it, and from that he guessed that the Konochine were a very small people indeed, certainly not much larger than five feet tall. A hundred feet back from the mesa's rim the land had been painstakingly cleared of anything larger than a pebble, and it seemed that whatever buildings had formed the outer rim of the concentric circles, all had their backs to one of the most spectacular views in the Southwest—flatland to the east, all the way to Texas, mountains to the north and west, a mixture to the south. Somber colors, few spots of discernible green, and combined with the voice of the wind that buffeted him lightly, it seemed less a desert than an alien terrain.

No, he thought. No, it's a graveyard, and he could almost feel the Konochine ghosts wandering about, watching him from behind what remained of their lives.

A noise, then, and he hurried back to the chimney mouth where Annabelle was just scrabbling for a handhold. He took her wrist and pulled her out, dusted her off, and stood silently with her while she took in the village.

"It's spooky," she said after a full minute of staring.

"I noticed. Nothing moves but the grass."

She sat on a flat-topped rock and draped her hands over her knees, her knapsack between her legs. Staring at the ends of the ladder tied to thick stakes, she seemed to Lincoln suddenly more Indian than Anglo, and when she saw his look, she grinned.

"I was going to tell you before, back at the arroyo, but we were interrupted. My mother and Peter were the reason my father eventually divorced her. After Loraleen was born, they weren't supposed to have any more children. Then I came along, right after they came out here on vacation. It took her husband three years to get up enough courage to throw her out for consorting with the natives." A laugh, bright and without regret. "She was a lot like Loraleen, if you can imagine it."

"So Peter did the proper thing and married your mother."

She nodded. "He has this ridiculous sense of right, if you know what I mean. I was their kid, Mother was without a husband, so it followed that I had to have a father, the real father. Peter also had the ranch, which didn't hurt."

The stake ropes creaked, and Wolf's head popped out of the hole. "Greetings from the underworld," he said.

Lincoln helped him, and said, "How'd you do it so fast?"

"Skill, tailor. Skill."

Lincoln looked at his hands rubbed raw, brushed them slightly on his jeans, and picked up his pack. "Well, I'm using the road on the way down, let me tell you that now. So let's get moving. I don't think I want to be up here all night."

Wolf agreed, and led them across the ceremonial field to a raised mound on the far side. There was a hole in its center, with the top of a ladder poking into the air. Wolf pointed. "It's down there, in the kiva."

"Kiva?"

"A chamber where the priests would go, to fast and find their visions. No one else but them was allowed down. Anyone who tried was asked to take a giant step off the edge."

Lincoln nodded, peered into the hole, and saw nothing but darkness. "I suppose your cultural heritage forbids you to go down there even now."

"Hell, no," Wolf said. "That's how I found the chest. But it's too heavy for me to carry up alone. You'll have to come down with me. Annabelle can wait here."

"Chauvinist," she accused, but neither did she argue.

Wolf took the ladder quickly, and Lincoln followed. It was too dark to see once they'd reached the bottom, but he didn't want to look around. Here, as well as up above, he could feel the dead and their sublime disapproval. The chest was at the ladder's foot, and though they almost dropped it several times in the hauling, they were back up in less than ten minutes. Neither looked at the other; there was no need.

"So," Annabelle said briskly. "This is it, huh?"

It looked like a pirate's chest to Lincoln as he knelt beside it, running a hand lightly across its rusted iron bands, the chips and gouges in the age-darkened oak. The rounded top seemed to have taken a number of blows from a sharp instrument, as though some-one had tried to open it long before the Konochine vanished. The lock was heavy, and run through with a stout chain. He tugged at it experimentally, then reached into his pack and pulled out his gun.

"Hey," Wolf said, backing away, "that's not one of the Mantos'."

"Right," he said, standing and moving to one side. "I prefer my own fun, thank you." And he fired twice, three times before the chain fell away and the lock unsnapped. But before the others could move in, he turned the gun on them and smiled. "I also prefer my own company sometimes. At least then I know where I stand."

"Lincoln!" Annabelle gasped.

"This isn't funny," said Wolf.

"No," he said readily, "but what is funny is how I always seem to be almost but not quite getting killed. I mean, it's really awfully strange, don't you think?"

"Lincoln," Annabelle pleaded, looking fearfully at the gun.

"Now you see, I know the Manto family, and I know damned well they aren't as incompetent as they have been on this little tour here—unless something shorted out in their genes along the way, which wouldn't surprise me, but I don't think that's the case. So on the way up I did a little thinking to keep my mind off my possible demise. You want to hear it?"

Annabelle shook her head, then nodded, then shook her head again, then dropped onto one of the steps and spread her hands in confusion. Wolf, on the other hand, remained where he was.

"Briefly," said Lincoln, "I figure it this way—Peter here discovers the legend of Knight in the stories of his people, knows the trouble Farren has and how gullible he is for anything that would help him save his life. So he lets on about it, convinces Farren it has to be found, and convinces him as well that yours truly ought to fetch it. Yours truly gets roped into it, you'll excuse the expression, and con-tributes his back to the affair because Peter was right, that chest is a bitch to move around."

"No," Annabelle said. "That's silly, Lincoln. Peter didn't have to go through all that. He knew where it was. He could have gotten one of the hands to help him move it."

"Oh no," Lincoln said sadly. "No, he couldn't. Because the Mantos didn't want just one of the hands. They wanted me."

"Mantos?" Annabelle said, looking to Peter.

"To be honest," Lincoln said, waving Wolf back with the gun, "I didn't figure it out until just a few minutes ago. I think, you see, what threw me is that Peter suspects there's more in that chest than a horse's tail."

"Mantos?" Annabelle said.

"Farren said it was woven together with gold thread and baubles. Knowing the Arabs, my guess is those baubles are worth a fortune."

Wolf kept backing up.

Lincoln beckoned Annabelle, had her grab the other end of the chest's rounded lid, and lift.

"See, the horse's hair would be probably long gone, even out here in the desert. But what would be left—"

The lid screeched on its iron hinges, fell back with a dust-raising thud, and Annabelle licked her lips as she looked cautiously inside.

"Not bad, huh?" he said, glaring Wolf into freezing.

"Lincoln."

"I'm sorry," he said truthfully. "I didn't mean to hurt you."

"Lincoln."

"What now?"

"Look."

He did.

"Well, son of a bitch," he said. "Damnit, Annabelle, you didn't tell me about this."

FIFTEEN

Annabelle gasped in wonderment as Lincoln reached into the chest and pulled the object out. Wolf took an involuntary step forward, stopping only when he saw the barrel of Linc's pistol remind him of his status.

"Lincoln, it's *real!*"

"Looks that way, doesn't it."

"My god, it's really real."

He held it by the end that was bound and braided into a tight, almost wood-hard grip six inches long, scarcely believing it himself. The rest of it, nearly three feet of it, was a complex spiraling of fine gold thread and Knight's intense black hair, and spaced regularly throughout were dozens of red stones. Rubies. Of all sizes, all of them polished, all of them flaring as the sun struck them. The color of the gold itself was deep, almost sullen, and cold when he ran a light finger down its length.

"I didn't believe it," Annabelle said quietly, leaning close and squinting, a hand out and drawn slowly back. "All this time, and I never really believed it."

Lincoln said nothing. He could see that both were quite understandably mesmerized by the talisman's beauty and strangeness, but he could not tell them about the sudden curious feeling that had crept into his hand and along his arm. It was much like the faint tingle of electricity, much like the deep thrumming of a powerful underground machine reverberating through one's soles, and it was like nothing he had ever experienced before. It was power, a power that made him instantly and silently ask for Upshire's forgiveness.

Without a single shred of proof, he was convinced that it would do everything the legends claimed.

He held it higher, level with his face, and saw that the gold was not simply spun and entwined about the strands of hair, but faceted as well by some artisan's skill long since forgotten. The facets mirrored the rubies, mirrored the sun, and masked the shadows he also saw lurking deep within it. It took no imagination to see how powerful Abadar had been in his times, and how much of that magic had been invested in his mount. It must have been, he thought, one hell of an animal.

"Lincoln?"

He blinked away the near trance that had infected him, and struggled to keep himself from grinning like a fool. "Yes?"

"Now what?"

He looked at Wolf, who had taken a seat on a rock and was watching him calmly. "Now we go back down, get back to the airport as fast as we can, and take this thing to your uncle."

"Oh."

He frowned at the tone of disappointment in her voice. "You have a better idea?"

"We could sell it," she suggested offhandedly. "Can you imagine what some museum would pay for this? Or some rich private collector? I could . . . we could be independently wealthy by the end of the month." She smiled dreamily. "Think of it, Lincoln, just think of it. No more shoveling out stables, no more tacos, no more worrying about whether the air-conditioning is going to break down and fry you in your bed." She looked up at him and sighed deeply. "Oh, brother."

"'Sure."

The wind came up then, warm and dry, and the gold sparked, the rubies fired as the tail turned slowly in his hand, back and forth, its colors reflecting on their faces, on the ground, in their eyes.

Suddenly, he snapped his arm down and held the tail behind him. Annabelle gave a small cry of despair, then staggered back as if she'd been struck. Her hands covered her eyes briefly, and lowered. Wolf rose, hands in his pockets.

"Gee," she said. "God, that's strong medicine."

He took a deep breath and blew it out in stages, lowered his gaze to the tips of his boots and shook his head. No wonder that priest had been so influential, and had been so brutally murdered when he could no longer heal because the Konochine wouldn't let him have his talisman. The damned thing was like a cobra just waiting for its victim to look into its eyes. The idea of that latent power now began to frighten him, and he quickly placed it back in the chest and slammed the lid shut.

"Do we leave now?" Annabelle asked.

"Eat first, leave second," he said, kneeling to open his knapsack. "And somewhere in there we're going to have to find something to cover that thing up or we'll be wandering around like zombies. We can't take the chest, it's too heavy, and we can't have it hanging out where everyone can see it."

"Okay," she said, and knelt beside him, pawing through her own sack to find the sandwiches she'd made that morning. When she held one up triumphantly, he took it, opened it, and offered her a silent toast with baked ham and cheese. She grinned. He grinned back.

And Peter Wolf leaned over the chest and rested the barrel of a gun softly against Linc's temple.

"Bang," he said. "You're dead."

"No," Lincoln said as he laid his own weapon on the ground beside him, "I'm stupid."

"Maybe," the Indian said agreeably, "but right now you're still alive, so don't tempt me to revert to the barbaric nature of my ancestors."

He gestured, and Lincoln backed away from the chest into the middle of the ceremonial plaza. Annabelle stood where she was, hands limp at her sides, and he wished that she would finally make up her mind whose side she was on. All this uncertainty was making him a nervous wreck.

Wolf dug into his knapsack and pulled out a length of rope which he threw to his daughter. She caught it, surprised, and was even more surprised when she was ordered to tie Linc's hands and feet. It was apparent that the man didn't consider her to be on anyone's side but her own and wasn't about to trust her. Linc admired his caution and deplored his sense of timing.

Wolf stood over her, then, while amid a spate of apologies and a few random but applicable curses, she bound his wrists, looped the rope around his ankles and effectively prevented him from doing anything but lying there on the hot, dusty grass. After she was finished, Wolf grabbed her arm and yanked her toward the kiva. Linc turned to watch, just in time to see the man clip her alongside the head and dump her into the underground room. Then he pulled up the ladder and dragged it to the mesa's rim, balanced it, and tipped it over with a gunhand salute. When he was assured it wouldn't stop until it reached the desert floor, he walked over to the chest and opened it.

"Hell of a way to treat your own daughter," Linc said.

Wolf shrugged. "She won't die. She'll find a way out, or you will, and you'll get down. Besides, she's too much like her mother. I didn't much care for her, either."

"Then why did you marry her?"

"She had a lot of land, Mr. Blackthorne. A lot of land. You may not think that's much, but this poor dumb Indian doesn't have a college education. That's sort of limiting when you're trying to make it in a world that doesn't want any part of you."

"That's awfully cold thinking, Peter."

"That's realistic, Blackthorne. Now why don't you just relax and think of a way you two can get out of your mess."

"You're pretty sure we will, aren't you?"

"You're clever, Mr. Blackthorne. You'll find a way."

"And when I do?"

Wolf took off his shirt, dropped it over the talisman, and picked the bundle up again. "Then all you have to do is find the road and hitchhike." He smiled. "Just stick out your thumb and show your legs. No problem."

Wonderful, he thought; the man's a Claudette Colbert fan.

He looked up at the sky, then, ducking his head away from the blinding blue and the white-hot sun. It was just close to noon, and all the shadows in the pueblo had retreated to the crumbling walls. Perspiration had already drenched his shirt and turned his hair into a skullcap, and though his gaze then fixed on the mouth of the kiva for several long seconds, he could hear no sound from within.

With a minimum of effort, Wolf proceeded to pick up the weapons, close the chest, and make sure the knapsacks had been tossed far out of reach. He disappeared for a while behind one of the buildings, and Lincoln took the opportunity to test Annabelle's knots. They were perfect. When he attempted to stretch the rope, he felt as if his wrists were going to be shredded and his ankles torn from his legs. That, he thought, is what you get when you get involved with a cowgirl.

Wolf returned, picked up his shirt, and walked to the ladder. Using the sleeves, he tied the bundle around his waist, stuck his gun in his belt and started down.

"Hey, Peter!"

Wolf paused, his expression amused.

"What if the Mantos didn't make it?"

"What if they didn't?" he said. "They're not the ones who want the tail, anyway."

"Tremain?"

Wolf nodded.

"And you know where he is."

Wolf nodded again.

"You going to give me a hint?"

Wolf laughed, hummed a few bars of "O Canada," and disappeared. The rope creaked and groaned against the stakes for a long time, and Lincoln couldn't help but stare at them, willing them to pry loose from the ground, praying that the rope would fray and eventually snap. But the movement gradually slowed, and he lost track of how much time passed before there was no movement at all.

Wolf was down, and the talisman with him.

Canada, he thought; that sonofabitch was still alive, and still in Canada.

A puzzled frown creased his brow. That didn't make much sense. Tremain Manto was not known for sending others to do his work for him. Especially not his kin. Either Wolf was trying to throw him off the trail, or there was yet something else nobody had told him about this whole mess.

A resigned shrug as best he could under the circumstances. And why shouldn't there be something else? Why should things be easy now?

Nuts.

Damn.

He turned then, and puffed his cheeks, checked the sky again in case there was a miracle storm on its way, and looked as best he could over his shoulder at the way Annabelle had trussed him. A sigh for her efficiency, and he rolled over until he was facing the kiva's mound. He called, listened, and shook his head at the wind as it gusted across the mesa, moaning in the ruins, raising brief clouds of smoky dust that seemed too much like the ghosts he'd imagined when he'd arived. A second call, and he cursed the wind when he thought he heard a faint reply.

A cloud drifted across the sun. It was white, thin, and served only to set a temporary haze in the air.

"Lincoln?"

His eyes closed in relief. "Are you all right?"

"Yes." It was eerie, that voice deepened by the mouth of the kiva, given a slight echo because of the chamber's size. "Are you going to get me out?"

"Annabelle—"

"It's dark down here, and my head hurts."

"Annabelle, listen, I—"

"Boy, you just don't know your own parents sometimes, you know it?"

He tried rolling closer so he wouldn't have to shout, but the rope burned into his wrists, and he hissed at the pain.

The heat intensified. He heard a faint buzzing in his ears.

"Lincoln?"

"Annabelle, I can't help you, for heaven's sake."

"Why? Are you still mad because of the lamp?"

"No, because you tied me up, that's why."

"Oh."

He shifted again, wincing at a stone that dug into his hip. A glance around the plaza, and he found himself staring at the ruined building Wolf had visited before he'd left. He wondered if the man had rigged a trap of some sort back there, ready to go off the moment either of them managed their escape. But there was nothing to see but the weather-pocked walls and the high weeds growing at the base, and he decided to ignore it until he was, in fact, free of his bonds.

Another painful look at the ropes, and he turned his right wrist slightly, flexed, and felt the knife slip smoothly out of its sheath.

He hadn't expected to be able to catch it; that would be asking too much. What he didn't expect was its striking a half-buried rock and caroming halfway across the grassy plot toward the tiered steps.

Not to mention burying itself in the grass so that he couldn't even see the blade reflecting the sun.

"Lincoln?"

"I'm working on it, I'm working on it."

"Lincoln, there are *things* down here."

"So?"

"I don't think they're friendly."

"What do they look like?"

"I don't know. They're staying back in the shadows. I'm here under the hole, where the sun's coming in."

"Then stay there." With a grunt he began inchworming his way along the ground, a process made all the more difficult because of the way his legs and arms were bent back, and because of the stones that dug into his skin through his clothes. "It'll be a while, though. You'll have to be patient."

"Loraleen."

He paused to shake the stinging perspiration from his eyes. "What?"

"Loraleen. She told me something else about you."

"What?"

"She said you were exciting." Annabelle did not sound as if she were pleased to know that.

He pushed again, pulled with his shoulder, pushed and dragged until he thought he would either pass out from the heat or lose one or both of his arms.

"I think I'll kill her."

Somehow he managed to turn himself so that he was facing the area where the knife had gone. His breathing was ragged, and the heat lay on him now like a flatiron.

"Maybe I could cut off her braids. She'd fall on her face and choke to death on her broken nose."

Sideways into the higher grass, the blades sharp-edged and drawing themselves across his face. He had to half-close his eyes to keep from being blinded, his open mouth taking in as much dust as air. Twice he gagged; twice more he choked when he swallowed something he could have sworn was an insect.

"Lincoln?"

"I'm still alive."

"Lincoln, I'm scared."

Two of us, he thought as he scanned the ground ahead, trying to see through the clumps of grass.

And when he saw it at last, its black grip seemingly melting into the ground, he called out to tell her.

"Then hurry up!"

He nodded, and ordered the pain to subside while he moved as quickly as he could, stirring the dust, rasping through the grass, until he was lying on an exposed table of rock level with the ground, and he was face to face with the blade.

And a pair of huge scorpions.

SIXTEEN

Lincoln held his breath.

The rock on which he lay baked through his shirt as though he were lying on a griddle.

The scorpions were at least four inches long and were poised on either side of the blade of the knife, one with its tail slightly arched over its back, the other apparently more relaxed. And they could not have been more than a foot away from the tip of his nose.

Had he been standing, they wouldn't have seemed quite so large or repulsive, but as close as they were, he could clearly see the entire length of their eight legs, the ponderous, crablike pincers waving in front of their jaws, and the sting that protruded from the bulbous tip of their tails. They were the color of dark sand, without any markings that he could see save for a covering along the back and tail of small dark hairs that gave them an appearance as menacing as any of the rattlers he'd encountered.

He knew there were different kinds of scorpions, and knew that not all of them injected deadly poison. But he had no idea which was which, no idea how much danger he was in now, or if the most he would receive was a painful sting and a few hours' discomfort.

One of them moved.

It began to scuttle toward him, and his lower lip sucked in between his teeth. There was no sound but Annabelle's increasingly concerned calls for his attention, and as much as he wanted to answer her, he knew that the wrong move would have him stung before he could jerk away.

It moved closer.

He could see the tiny black eyes lifeless and flat above the constantly working jaws, could see the sting trembling on its segmented stalk.

It reached his chin, and one pincer drifted over it, making the flesh tighten.

On the rock its legs made a faint scrabbing sound.

His lungs began to protest, and when he felt a veil of dizziness begin to slip over him, he released the air in as small a stream as he could, aiming it up and away from the creature as it traveled farther down his body, brushing against his chest as if searching for a way to get under the cloth.

The second scorpion moved.

He felt the first one probing at a gap between the buttons of his shirt. The pincer was hard, rough, and it was all he could do to keep from screaming.

The second scorpion, after darting to one side as if seeking a way around him, stopped directly in front of his eyes, and its tail was high now, in position to strike.

The wind gusted, the grass bending away, the harsh sandy dust coating his face.

He knew he wouldn't be able to wait much longer. If his nerves didn't give out and betray him with violent trembling, his lungs would require a deep breath that would spur the scorpions into action. He had to do something, and he couldn't roll back out of the way, not fast enough, not nearly fast enough to escape them if they pursued.

And he couldn't threaten them with any action of his own. Noises wouldn't work, and he certainly couldn't blow them away like the Big Bad Wolf. The blackjack was still in his hip pocket, Palmer's special concoction was in his knapsack somewhere back there in the ruins, and what in god's name was he thinking of when he didn't even have any hands to hold on to anything with?

The wind blew again, softer this time, and the second scorpion moved away, back toward the knife, across the hilt and into the grass where it disappeared.

Thank you, he said silently, and lowered his gaze to his chest.

The remaining creature was still there by his chest, still poking around at the gaps between buttons. It wasn't about to leave, and Lincoln could think of only one way to get rid of it. The problem was, if this was one of the deadly species, Annabelle was going to have a hell of a time getting out of the kiva on her own.

On the other hand, he wasn't going to just lie here and let the scorpion make up his mind for him.

He closed his eyes.

The scorpion slipped a pincer into the shirt.

He slowly arched his back and stuck out his chest.

The scorpion's tail lowered just a bit.

Then Lincoln shouted as loud as he could and rolled over, pinning the scorpion between his sternum and the rock, and began to grind side to side, yelling, nearly screaming, and waiting for the feel of the sting in his flesh.

A full minute later he rolled over with a jerk, and gulped for air, turned his head and saw the crushed body of the scorpion smeared across the rock. A look to his chest at the dark stain on his shirt, and he swallowed the bubble of bile that rose in his throat before sidling quickly to the knife and grabbing the blade between his teeth. He did not look for the dead scorpion's companion; if it came, it came, and there was nothing he could do about it. Instead, he continued to crawl crabwise until he reached the steps and found a gap between the crumbling rock. It took nearly ten minutes, but he was able to prop the hilt in, then turn and begin to saw through the rope.

The sun made his head spin.

He heard voices on the wind, children singing a song in a language he did not understand; he heard footsteps behind him, always behind him, but every time he looked, there was no one in sight; he heard water splashing down a fall; he heard the blood slowing in his veins.

The rope would not give.

Annabelle no longer called him.

He saw between the buildings the edge of the mesa, and beyond it a magnificent pink galleon sailing before the wind; he saw a penguin strutting out of the chimney, a pipe in its beak, a briefcase in one flipper; he saw the cavalry riding out of the shadows; he saw Tremain Manto standing a foot above the ground, his face white with scars from the acid he'd thrown, his mouth wide in a silent laugh that thundered across the desert.

His lips cracked, and his eyes felt burned away, and it wasn't until he fell backward that he realized the rope had snapped apart and his hands were finally freed.

The moment he knew he wasn't bound anymore, he sagged against the steps and passed out. When he regained consciousness only a few seconds later, he worked with numbed fingers on his ankles until at last he could gather the rope to him and prop himself up. He knew he couldn't walk just yet, but the idea that he would be able to soon was enough to make him laugh softly to himself, enough to let him breathe without hurting, enough at last to force him to stand. His knees almost buckled. His left arm snapped out to give him balance, and he tightroped across the plaza to the mouth of the kiva. There, with a groan, he dropped to his knees and looked down.

"Annabelle?"

He could see the shaft of sunlight reaching to the kiva floor, and the ladder of dust trapped by the beam.

"Annabelle!"

The ground was disturbed just below the opening, but when he leaned in as far as he could, he could see no sign of a body, or a woman sitting or lying down.

"Annabelle!"

A scraping noise then, and he waited until at last she staggered into view, her blouse covered with layers of grey dirt, her hands black with it, her hair tangled and almost white.

"What . . ." He shook his head. "What were you doing, trying to dig your way out?"

"You got a better idea?"

He held up the rope, and she smiled so broadly he thought her cheeks would split in half.

With the rope around his waist, he lowered the other end down and leaned back as a brace while she climbed agilely up and out, swearing at the blinding sun, then seeing him for the first time and demanding to know what had happened, why he hadn't answered

her when she'd called. He told her succinctly and was perversely
pleased to see her grimacing at the end.

"You know," she said, helping him to his feet and keeping an arm
around his waist, "I'm really glad this is over." They staggered together across the plaza toward the chimney mouth. "I mean, it's a
shame the bad guys won and all, but I'll tell you the truth, Lincoln, I
could sell that ranch tomorrow, and if I invest the proceeds pretty
carefully, I could do all right for a long time. I mean, I wouldn't be
rich or anything, but I wouldn't be on the dole, either."

He told her where he'd seen Wolf toss the knapsacks, then waved
her down beside him when she returned. Her expression was sol-
emn, even considering their predicament, and when he asked her
what was wrong, she was reluctant to answer.

"C'mon, Annabelle, there can't be any secrets now."

"I found out what Peter was doing back there."

"Oh?"

"Scorpions," she said, not meeting his gaze. "There's a nest or
colony or whatever you call it back there by the rocks. He was
stirring them up."

He grunted.

"I'm so ashamed."

And she astounded him by suddenly breaking into tears. He could
do nothing else then but put his arm around her shoulder and hold
her until she was finished, until she had wiped her eyes with her
sleeve and regained her composure.

If nothing else, then, he knew at last which side she was on.

"Now what?" she said, sheepishly wiping off his face with the
other sleeve.

"Now we go down."

She looked at the ladder. "That way?"

He considered the steep trail, the wind, the possibility of falling,
and nodded.

"Then what?"

"Then we heroically battle our way across the desert during the
cool hours of the evening, find civilization, find a car, and find Peter
Wolf before he has a chance to do anything with our treasure."

She held up a hand. "Wait a minute, wait a minute. I thought this was all over."

"*You* thought it was over," he said grimly. "I'm not about to let that man get away. Not now."

"I don't get it."

He cupped her chin with one hand and tried to make her see into his mind. "Annabelle, Tremain Manto is going to be awfully ticked off when Peter shows up with Knight's magic, and without me. That means Tremain will come after me himself. And that means I won't be able to go home without wondering if there's a trap on the plane or in my house or . . . well, you see what I mean?"

"I see it," she said grumpily. "I don't like it, but I see it."

"Besides, has it occurred to you that helping me will make your uncle very, very happy? And if he's very, very happy, you may find that—"

Annabelle strapped on her knapsack, helped him on with his own, and started down the ladder. He watched until she was out of sight, then wiped his hands on his thighs and followed. He thought of nothing on the way down except how great it would be to be down in the first place, and he surprised himself into grunting when his feet, instead of finding another rung, struck solid rock instead.

Annabelle was waiting for him, and she led him from the cave and through the brush to the outside.

"Incredible," he said, looking over the desert floor.

"What is?"

"It's flat."

"Yeah, so?"

"It's flat, and I'm not, which means I didn't fall, which means we might as well get out of the sun and get comfortable. There's a heck of a long walk ahead, and I've got a lot of resting to do."

She laughed, and volunteered to fill their canteens from the stream under the trees. Graciously, he permitted her to do it while he returned to the cool of the cave and propped himself against one wall. There was always the remote possibility that Wolf had linked up with Storm and Rain, and they might convince Wolf to return for him. But he doubted it. Once the two brothers saw all that gold, and all those rubies, they would think of nothing else but how pleased Tremain would be. The recriminations would come later, and by that time he would either be dead in the desert, or—

"Lincoln?"

"In here," he called gaily.

"Lincoln, you'd better get out here."

On the other hand, he thought as he pushed his way out, they might also come back to finish the job in revenge for his leaving them out there without protection.

"What?" he said.

Annabelle was staring off to the west, and pointing at a dim figure making its way toward them. He shaded his eyes, looked, and looked again.

"Annabelle, that looks like a man out there."

"Yes."

"That man is on a dune buggy."

"I know."

"I think," he said, "we don't have to walk."

"But what if he isn't friendly?"

He didn't know how to explain it to her, so he didn't try. But he knew something was up since that was the only desert rat he'd ever heard of who wore a Gucci sombrero with a wobbly cluster of plastic grapes.

SEVENTEEN

The trip back to the Bannon ranch was something less than luxurious, but Lincoln supposed he was lucky to be getting back at all. Because he wanted to be sure he could see anyone following, as well as those who might come at them across the desert, he ignored the protests of his already battered limbs and sat behind the seats in back, holding on to the support braces with both hands and praying that his organs would not jolt too far out of position.

Over the noise of the buggy's engine, then, he learned that Old Alice could not stand not being in on the action, especially when the declared alternative was going to the movies, again, with the old fart in the white beard. Without telling anyone, including Farren Upshire, and using, she said, the second meager installment of her life savings, she booked the first flight she could, tracked down the location of the ranch and, eventually, the location of the Konochine Pueblo.

Though Annabelle asked in astonished admiration how she'd managed it—while at the same time eyeing her and her sombrero skeptically—Lincoln did not. Experience had taught him well the habits of his old friend. He knew that despite her apparent and scrupulously cultivated fragility, Old Alice could follow a white rabbit in a snowstorm a month after the fact and never get her feet wet or catch a simple cold. Instead, he asked her if, in her insane desire to accommodate her death wish, she had learned where the Manto brothers had gone with Peter Wolf.

"Lincoln," Annabelle admonished, "for heaven's sake, she only just got here."

"Howatoon," Alice yelled as she swerved sharply to avoid a jackrabbit, and deftly straightened her sombrero.

"Where's that?" he and Annabelle asked in unison.

"Last I heard, somewhere in the Yukon."

Annabelle blanched and swallowed, and didn't move or speak again until she pointed when they reached the entrance to the Bannon homestead; and she kept her silence until they were in the kitchen and she was making the largest lunch she could from the stores she had.

None of the hands were around. Lincoln, in response to an unspoken request, made a quick reconnaissance of the grounds. Though nothing had been damaged that he could see, he found what looked suspiciously like hastily dug graves beyond the back fence, but decided that Annabelle had enough to cope with without knowing that now.

"We'll leave first thing in the morning," he said after the meal was done and they were in the living room. He nodded to Annabelle, and Old Alice glowered.

"I ain't going back to that old fart," she declared.

"Well, you're not coming with us, either."

Alice opened her purse, pulled out a compact, and examined the damage done her face by the desert sun. "You know where Howatoon is?"

"I don't even know what it means."

"I know what it means, and I know where it is."

Annabelle, who had pushed herself into the corner of the couch and was watching the two with an increasingly bewildered expression, cleared her throat. It was meant to be a signal to Lincoln, to be gentle with the old bat and not hurt her feelings. After all, she did rescue them from the pueblo, and the heat.

Alice smiled at her as she pulled a gleaming, jade-etched .45 magnum from the purse. "Don't worry, dear, I know how to take care of myself."

Annabelle opened her mouth to argue, closed it again when the barrel swung innocently past her midsection to vanish back into the purse. She shrugged. She pulled her legs up under her and took hold of her ankles. Then she couldn't quite stop herself from yawning.

Lincoln, who had taken an armchair on the other side of the coffee table, leaned forward, his forearms resting on his thighs. "Alice, don't be silly. I know you can take care of yourself, but I can't let you go. This isn't a lark. We're talking about the Mantos here, and you remember what happened the last time we were graced with the dubious pleasure of their company."

Alice rolled her eyes.

Annabelle sniffed, and yawned again.

"Alice, don't argue with me. Just tell me how—"

"No," Alice said, folding her arms decisively over her chest. "You can't do it alone, Blackie. You know that. You know how it is, and you know Manto."

He did, all too well, and when he saw the determination in the woman's eyes, he knew, too, that it was useless to continue the discussion. Alice was more than capable of letting him go off blind, and he supposed it would be better to have her and her pet .45 along than to end up wandering through the Yukon for the rest of his life.

Later, when they finally caught up with Manto and Wolf, he would consider ditching her, to keep her out of trouble.

Annabelle yawned again.

Old Alice clucked, took the girl's arm, and together they headed for the bedrooms at the back of the house. Lincoln turned the chair around and watched the sun over the mountains, and for a moment the scene gave him a forbidding sense of déjà vu. So much so that a chill walked his spine, and settled on the back of his neck like the cold point of a dagger.

Five minutes later Alice returned and stood in front of him.

"You trust that girl?"

"Nope," he said truthfully. "Some. Not all."

"Good. She'll do fine as long as we don't give her cause to examine our backs." When he didn't take the bait, she set her hands on her hips and leaned closer. "You been thinking about the Mantos?"

He nodded.

"You scared?"

He nodded again.

A deep, noisy breath, and she straightened. "Good. That's a healthy attitude. It keeps a man honest and breathing." A hand reached up to adjust the grapes. A sandal tapped on the floor. She pursed her lips and whistled silently. "I give up," she said at last. "You find that horse's tail you were looking for?"

"Yep."

She blinked her surprise. "Does it do what the Jersey blimp thinks?"

"Never had a chance to test it." He said nothing about the uncanny sensation of power he'd had when he had handled it on the mesa. "On the other hand, it could make a lot of people awfully rich." He described the intricate gold twining and its nest of rubies. "If Tremain's looking for a way to finance some project of his, this will do it, without question."

Alice turned away abruptly with a hissing inhalation, and Lincoln was puzzled. But he didn't interrupt her while she hummed, tapped a pensive finger on her hip, hummed a bit more, and started to pace around the room; he only waited, not liking her reticence. This wasn't like her, and it could only mean she knew something else.

Something, he thought, he wasn't going to like one single bit.

Finally, she returned to the window. "Godawful country out there," she said.

"It has its own beauty."

"Sure," she muttered. "Like Palmer in the nude. You ever see Palmer in the nude?"

"Nope."

"Me neither. Word gets around. It's not a pleasant sight."

"Alice, what's up?"

She whirled on him and tossed a piece of paper in his lap. He stared, picked it up, and saw it was a telegram.

"From a friend of mine in the Mounties," she said grimly.

"You got your man?" he said with a smile.

"I always do. So do they."

"Alice—"

"Read it, Blackie, and we'll talk in the morning."

He read it. He read it a second time, and the chill walked again.

Alice nodded once and, as she walked away, mumbled something about getting her beauty rest. Lincoln didn't try to stop her. He only glanced a third time at the message and let the paper fall to the floor.

It was indeed from the Royal Canadian Mounted Police—a verification of an apparent query Alice had sent her friend before she'd left.

The police left no room for doubt—eight months ago Tremain Manto had been killed in a gunfight with a squad of Mounties. He was pronounced dead by three different doctors, two coroners, and a detective sergeant. His body was taken by a friend of the family's and never seen again. Further doubt was erased in the description of the man's wounds—five bullets in the chest, three in the left leg, two in the right, four almost evenly spaced across his forehead.

He would like to see you again, Storm Manto had said. *He's going to get himself all better.*

The cabin was deceptively small. Little more than a hunter's modest lodging, it completely and effectively disguised the underground rooms which were large and comfortable, save for the last. Here, in the center of the hard earthen floor, was a large cast-iron caldron. A witch's caldron. Bubbling, steaming, hanging from a heavy black chain over a galloping fire in a pit six feet deep. The flames were the only illumination in the room, and the shadows he could see beyond the caldron never remained in one place for more than a few seconds at a time. He was not bound, but there was no place to go, no way to escape. There was only the shadows, and the fire, and the hissing from the caldron.

And there was Tremain Manto.

He was speaking, but Lincoln could not hear him.

He was laughing, but Lincoln could only see the white of his teeth.

He was pointing to the caldron and the acid foaming inside, and somehow Lincoln managed to look down at his hand to the glass vial he held. He had no idea where he'd gotten it, or who had given it to him, but he knew that it was the only way he was going to leave this place alive.

Manto ordered someone to take his arms and bind him, lift him on a pulley over the caldron.

Lincoln ducked away from the grasping hands, his wrist knife snapping out into his palm. The blade sank into a woman's stomach, and she screamed without a sound. A young man lunged for him, and Lincoln slashed him across the chest, shoved him into the wall, and turned just as Tremain stalked around the pit.

A second young man leapt out of the darkness.

Lincoln struck out with his boot, and the man staggered back. Tremain reached desperately for him, but the edge of the pit was steaming with spilled acid, slippery, and the young man screamed once, soundlessly, before falling in.

The flames rose in a silent rush.

The acid snapped over the side, landing on Tremain's arms, causing his shirtsleeves to smolder.

Lincoln moved. Slowly. Too slowly. As if he were watching a grainy, ancient film, he saw his arm swing up, saw the acid in the vial stream green and gold into the air, and saw at last Manto fling up his hands to protect himself.

Too late. Much too late.

The acid landed on his cheeks, and instantly there was the stench of burning flesh, and his skull exposed to the hellish light from the flames.

Lincoln turned to run, and a hand grabbed his shoulder.

He bolted from the chair as if scalded; a yell caught in his throat when he blinked and saw Annabelle moving away from him. There was fear in her eyes, and concern, and he managed a shaky smile as he sank on the windowsill and took several deep breaths to calm the race of his heart.

"Bad dream?"

"Yeah, you could say that."

"You hungry?"

He realized, then, the room was filled with a soft bronze light, and when he looked over his shoulder, he saw the nightsky giving way slowly to dawn. Damn, he thought; he'd spent the entire night in a damn chair when there were a dozen beds to be had. His hands scrubbed his face dryly, and he groaned loudly when the aches in his legs and arms erupted with dull thudding.

"I think I'll die now and be done with it," he said, standing and walking stiffly in a circle.

"I have a better idea." She took his elbow and guided him through a door in back. "The master bathroom's down there. Take a shower. Soak in the tub. Make yourself presentable, and I'll have something waiting on the table."

"Alice?"

Annabelle laughed. "She's been up for hours already. Walking around outside. She says she wants to find out what the attraction is here."

"Insatiable curiosity," he told her. "The woman is never satisfied."

"And I take it she's going?"

"Absolutely," he said. "If we try to keep her away, we won't live to see lunch."

Annabelle wasn't certain how much he was exaggerating, and Lincoln wasn't about to give her a clue. A wink, a touch of thanks to her arm, and he hurried off down the hall, trying several doors before he found what he wanted.

"I don't believe it," he whispered as she stepped inside and closed the door behind him.

It was a bathroom easily as large as his entire Inverness apartment, with an earthen brown carpet so rich and cool it was like walking barefoot in a meadow. Along the far wall, the black marble tub was sunken three steps below the level of the floor; on the lefthand wall the four-headed shower was in a green marble stall like a walk-in closet, and there were four red marble basins aligned on the righthand, pink-tiled wall, each with its own mirror, each with gold faucets in the shape of diving dolphins.

The lighting was recessed, a glow so gentle it was almost like daylight. When in experiment he switched the light off, the room fell into a darkness very nearly absolute.

Quickly, he flicked the switch again, then stripped, filled the tub, and sank in before the hot water could tell him he was being lobstered. The steam rose in streamers around him. His arms and legs and chest and back thanked him with a sigh. It was heaven, and he wondered if Palmer could rig him something like this back in New Jersey. The tub was long enough to stretch out in, wide enough for three people across, and had at either end a padded support for one's head and neck, so he could virtually float without bothering to hold on to the side.

This, he decided, would be the perfect place to retire. Not the state, only the bathroom. With a few willing and attractive ladies to pander to his fantasies, enough junk food to last him forever, and only the best—

He frowned and looked to his right.

Something had moved on the carpet by the door.

Carefully, he knelt on the tub's submerged bottom step. The rising steam made him squint and bat at the air, and the moment his arm moved, so did something else.

It was eight or nine inches long, and it was triplets, front and back segments so dark they were almost black. The longest, ugliest centipedes he had ever seen—and if memory served, they were poisonous as well.

When his arm lowered to splash gently back into the water, the center one reared, and the others started for him.

EIGHTEEN

His yell was enough to bring somebody running, but he wasn't about to wait to see if the centipedes could swim. He grabbed for an oversized towel on the rack by his head, rolled it swiftly into a flabby baseball bat and pressed his back against the cold tiled wall. Immediately the first two reached the tub's rim, he swung and knocked them aside, yelled again, and dashed across the carpet. The door opened just as he reached it, and he shouted a warning as he barreled through, putting an arm around Annabelle's waist and propelling her out with him. She gasped as she slammed against the corridor wall, but Lincoln turned instantly and pulled the door to.

"I am struck," he said, "by the variety of killers you have here in the desert."

Then he strode into the nearest bedroom, wrapped the towel around his waist and sat on the bed. His legs quivered, and he found it difficult to take a breath; the air was cold, yet perspiration beaded on his forehead.

There was a knock on the door.

Annabelle poked her head in, poked in an arm and tossed his clothes onto the bed. "I know," she said. "I didn't tell you about them, either."

"Could they have killed me?"

"It wouldn't have been nice."

He gave her a wan smile and waved her away, then climbed up onto the mattress where he could see the floor in all directions, and dried himself off, dressed, and waited a full five minutes before he was sure it was safe to walk again.

Once back in the living room, he told them all to pack, fetched his own knapsack from the foyer, and took out the vial Palmer had given him. He studied it a moment, peered down toward the kitchen, then slipped it into his shirt pocket.

Alice returned first, lugging a small briefcase. "I travel light," she explained to his wondering look. "And I checked a map. Blackie, do you have any idea where the Yukon is?"

"North," he said.

"Yeah. About two thousand miles worth."

"There are planes."

"Right. Pulled by eight tiny reindeer."

Annabelle joined them, snapping closed a knapsack, and after locking the ranchhouse up, they took the dune buggy back to the airport in Albuquerque. Lincoln hated the stares, Annabelle ignored them, and Old Alice spent most of her time waving as if she were in a presidential procession.

The first flight was to Denver.

The second, the next day, took them to Edmonton, with a change in Helena.

Alice noted that the planes were getting progressively smaller.

Annabelle noted that the mountains they crossed were getting progressively higher.

Lincoln kept his comments to himself. He was busy trying to locate a flight to Whitehorse, the Yukon's capital, which was, he figured, at least another thousand miles, give or take. He also kept an eye out for the Mantos, giving them enough credit to know that he would probably be right on their tail. Peter Wolf might have thought he was properly taken care of, but if Tremain had taught his sons anything, it was never to underestimate the stubbornness of a fool tailor.

By the end of the second day in Alberta, after a phone call or two and a chunk of Alice's life savings, he had arranged for a private plane to take them in three long legs to their destination. Alice protested the cost, Annabelle the inconvenience, and he shut them both up by reminding them of what had happened when he'd flown out from Dallas.

Then he introduced them to the pilot.

"My goodness," said Old Alice, and reached for her compact.

"You're kidding," said Annabelle, and reached for her drink.

"You couldn't," Lincoln said, "be in better hands than his."

They were sitting in a small bar at the edge of town, next to a motel where Lincoln had taken rooms. The bar's walls were of dark wood and moose heads, elk heads, deer heads, and a bobcat, and in the corner by the men's room was a stuffed, standing polar bear with a basket on one paw for the attendant's tips. Though it was late, there were few customers, most of them part of a construction gang. Boisterous, playing the jukebox, they stayed at the curved bar when it was clear the dark-haired lady was with the man in the black denims.

The booth was the last before the polar bear, its backs high and the table worn smooth by thousands of forearms. A small lamp on the wall cast more shadows than light, and once they were served, they were left quite alone.

"Don't worry," Lincoln said about the man on his left. "He knows the mountains around here like the backs of his hands."

"He's wearing gloves," Alice noted, knocking back her beer and banging the glass on the table to order another.

The pilot laughed, and Annabelle cringed—the sound was like the cry of a forlorn gander.

"What do you say, Pierre?" Lincoln said, lowering his voice in case the polar bear had ears. "Can we do it without being noticed?"

Pierre Requin lifted his shoulders in an expressive and meaningless shrug. He was at least Old Alice's age, but his craggy features were etched more sharply on his dark-skinned face because of exposure to the winter's winds, the summer's sun, and a handful of knife fights that had left their marks under each of his eyes. His hands were large and gnarled, his white hair in a crewcut he kept lifting with a palm, and when he opened his fleece-lined leather jacket, it was evident that his size came not only from the rack.

"I been doing that route for half a century, fifty year, maybe, Linc," he said quietly. "I can't promise a thing, except we don't dare land in Whitehorse. They'll be watching, maybe they be waiting."

"You married?" Alice asked.

Lincoln touched the man's arm. "You don't have to do this," he said. "You know that."

Requin shrugged again, this time with a smile. "You a liar, Linc."

"Any kids?" Alice inquired.

"You don't owe me anything, Pierre," he insisted gently. "But if you're going to play the hero . . ." He shrugged, and smiled, and looked to Annabelle, whose expression was flickering back and forth between dismay and bewilderment. "You have a question?"

Pierre laughed and took a long drink from his mug. "She be wondering, my friend, if this old coot can walk, much less get a plane off the ground."

Annabelle blushed.

"How about an apartment?" Alice probed.

Requin finally noticed her, and studied her so long and so intently that she began to preen without moving, studying him in turn from under the sombrero's brim. Then he finished his beer, ordered two more, and toasted her silently. She nodded. He nodded. She flipped back her sombrero and batted her eyelids. He doffed his fur hat and grinned broadly.

"Well," Lincoln said enthusiastically, "it looks as if we're all set, then."

Old Alice ignored him.

Requin hushed him with a brusque gesture.

Lincoln leaned over the table and beckoned Annabelle to do the same. "I think," he said, "we're in trouble here."

"Why? I think it's cute."

" 'Cute' isn't the word for it when Alice gets a notion to lure a man into her clutches. I've known Pierre for a long time, and I don't think even he has a chance."

She patted his cheek. "You have no romance in your soul, Mr. Blackthorne."

"The hell I don't," he said testily, shifting so the edge of the table would stop digging into his stomach. He glared once at the elderly couple and was about to lean back when she took his arm and pulled him even closer.

"You trust him?" she whispered, nodding toward Requin, who

was showing Old Alice how an Eskimo dentist had preserved most of his teeth.

"As much as I trust anybody," he answered.

"But he's so . . . so old."

"So is Alice."

"Yes, but . . ." She frowned. "Lincoln, I'm worried."

"About losing the ranch?"

She scowled then, and for a second he thought she was going to slap him. "No. About you. About me. This Manto family, they're not nice people."

"What about Peter? You keep forgetting him."

The moment he mentioned her father, he knew it was a mistake, and he knew she hadn't forgotten a single thing the man had done. Her brow creased, her dark eyes became flint, and her mouth set so tightly her lips nearly vanished. He could almost feel the chill, could hear her breathing slowly as if stoppering her temper, and he thought not for the first time that Annabelle Bannon was about as predictable as New England weather. Things had been so calm between them lately, he had just about forgotten the tricks she had pulled, and he wondered then if she had finally given up her plans to get Farren's farm.

Suddenly, he doubted it.

Going with him now, he decided, was only another way to reach her goal; and if in reaching it she had to move a few people out of the way, he also didn't doubt she'd do it without a qualm, though she'd have class enough at least to smile.

"You two gonna kiss or what?" Old Alice demanded loudly. "It ain't a private party, y'know."

Annabelle blinked at the intrusion, and Lincoln did the only gentlemanly thing he could think of—he put a hand on the back of her head, drew her close, and kissed her. And he didn't pull away until she bit his lower lip, which wasn't, he noted, her immediate reaction.

Another round of beers, and Lincoln excused himself, pushed his way past the polar bear into the men's room, and leaned against the wall. A moment later Pierre walked in.

"Crazy lady," he said, rinsing his hands at the sink.

"She's all right," Lincoln assured him. "She just likes sombreros."

"Not her, the other one," Pierre corrected. "I see it in her eyes. She's not a good one, Linc. She is trouble, for sure."

"For the Mantos, I hope."

"Maybe you think so."

They returned to the booth, paid the bill, and left. On the pavement outside Requin gave them directions to the airfield he'd be using, gave them the time, and sauntered off. Alice watched him intently, set her sombrero rakishly on her head, and followed. Annabelle took his arm and guided him toward their hotel.

They had just reached the entrance when suddenly Lincoln stopped, looked over his shoulder, and frowned.

"What's the matter?" she asked nervously, one hand dipping into the pocket of her jacket.

"I just thought of something."

He stood there silently, closing first one eye, then the other, as if testing his focus. Then, with a muttered oath, he told Annabelle to wait in her room, and he headed back to the bar, pushed in the door, and ignored the startled complaint of the bartender when he strode to the back and stood in front of the stuffed bear.

He was right.

When they were sitting in the booth next to it, the creature's eyes were light brown.

As far as he knew, polar bears' eyes were black.

"Hey, Mac, what the hell . . . ?" the bartender said.

They were the only two left, and Lincoln reached into his pocket, pulled out some money blindly, and tossed it behind him. When the barkeep lunged for it, he took a step closer to the bear and punched it in the stomach as hard as he could. The bartender scuttled in a hurry behind the register when a muffled groan broke from the polar bear's mouth. But he didn't do a thing when Lincoln punched it again, and a third time, before dusting off his hands and heading for the door.

"Get it out of the draft before it catches pneumonia," he said, left and did his best not to run to the hotel.

The night clerk eyed him sleepily. He nodded, hurried to the elevator bank, and punched the button for the fourth floor. Then he took the fire stairs down to the third, knocked on Annabelle's door, and when she opened it, he pushed his way in.

"Don't argue, and don't get unpacked," he said, forcing the inner door that connected their rooms. "Put your coat back on. We're leaving. Tonight."

"Now? Tonight?"

The door gave, and he grabbed his knapsack, checked for his cosh, knife, and gun, and returned just as she hefted her own bag to her shoulder.

"Now," he said.

"But Lincoln—"

Grabbing her arm, he pulled her into the hallway, looked at the indicator lights over the elevators, and pushed her into the fire stairwell. His urgency was catching, and she needed no prompting to take the concrete steps two at a time, slamming into the lobby and slowing with a shy grin, taking his arm and laughing softly. Lincoln kissed her quickly, and they staggered to the counter where the desk clerk was watching. He didn't blink when they checked out, didn't utter a word when they paid cash instead of using a credit card, and didn't try to follow when they stumbled into the street and suddenly began running.

"Where are we going?" she asked when they veered around a corner.

"Requin's place."

"But Alice is there!"

"She'll understand, just trust me," he said, took her arm and pulled her into an alley between two high brick buildings. They raced through a maze of garbage cans and empty cartons, veered left at the end, and came out on a narrow street whose facade made him wonder if this part of town had seen the light of day since the last gold rush farther north. The faces of the buildings were mostly wood and native stone, and there were no cars parked at the curb. Though no rain had fallen since their arrival, the street was damp and reflected the streetlamps in unnerving colors.

The only sound was the sound of their running.

Another alley, another block the same as the one they'd just left, and he headed for a doorway over which flashed a narrow neon sign. All it said was "Hotel," and just as he reached for the doorknob, a shot echoed down the empty street, and Annabelle fell into his arms.

NINETEEN

Lincoln grabbed Annabelle around the waist and kicked the door open with his heel, dragging her in behind him as quickly as he could. The darkwood lobby was empty; the brass trim on the wainscoting gleamed like polished stars in the light of the green-shaded lamps affixed to the walls. Annabelle moaned, and he lowered her to the worn carpet, at the same time reaching into his jacket to pull out his gun.

With his aim kept at the door, then, he looked down and tried to find evidence of the wound she'd received. But there was no tear in the jacket or in the jeans that he could see, and when he bent closer, he could see no blood at all. He was about to lower the gun and turn her over when she coughed suddenly and snapped open her eyes.

"Damn," she muttered, looked up and sniffed. "They ought to make those steps a bit higher, or lower. I could've killed myself, you know it?"

It took him a moment to understand, then he groaned himself and yanked her to her feet, scarcely listening as she complained about tripping . . . and what the hell was he talking about, somebody shot at them?

There was a magnificent stag's head on the wall in front of them, and under it the arched entrance to the Hotel's bar. As he hoped, the bartender was off duty, and the only customers were Old Alice and Requin canoodling in the far corner. Annabelle thought it was rather sweet; Lincoln offered no opinion, but rather shoved her through the maze of tables and didn't much care how many chairs he was knocking over.

When Alice and Pierre finally glanced up and saw him rushing in, they were on their feet without a question. Alice paid the bill; Requin yanked on his fur hat.

"How many?" he asked, pushing them toward the back kitchen. "No telling. A lousy shot, though."

"Didn't you shoot back?" Alice asked Annabelle.

"Shoot back? I didn't even know they were shooting front, for god's sake."

"Great," she muttered. "You must be one heck of a cowgirl."

The kitchen staff consisted of an obese woman in a chef's hat and white apron dozing on a counter, on a bed of flour. The noise they made never fazed her, and Requin giggled into one hand as he guided them around the ovens, the work islands, past a meat freezer and a microwave, and through a fire exit that let them out into an alley.

As they approached the street, Lincoln went ahead, half in a crouch with his gun out and ready. Requin and Annabelle took the rear, and he asked her if she knew who the sniper was.

"I don't know," she said, mincing around a pool of something liquid but not water. "All he said was something about a polar bear's eyes."

"A polar bear?"

She nodded.

Requin gave her one of his shrugs, and caught her arm just before she plowed into Old Alice, who was crouched behind Lincoln, who was wondering who'd elected him marshal of this parade.

The street was empty.

He could see no movement anywhere and could hear only the sound of traffic in the distance. He stepped out, his stomach tight, his legs ready to spring him back, but when nothing happened, he waved the others forward and they rushed toward the corner, keeping close to the buildings, the loudest noise the clatter of Old Alice's grapes.

Three blocks later they charged into an underground garage where Requin led them to a bright red pickup recently washed and polished.

"You have a sign for this thing?" Lincoln groused as he flung open the passenger-side door.

"It moves," the pilot told him, and then told him, "Ladies first."

"But there's not enough room!"

Requin pointed to a pile of burlap bags in back, handed him a thick blanket from under the front seat, and slid hastily behind the wheel. Lincoln glowered, then sighed and climbed onto the bed, pulled the blanket around him and was thrown against the cab wall when the old man gunned the truck backward out of its stall.

He closed his eyes.

There was no sense watching because there was nothing he could do about it, though he imagined that Old Alice was in her element at last.

He burrowed deeper into the corner once they reached the street, and kept an eye on the windows and rooftops while Requin kept an eye on the red lights he was ignoring. Linc had to admit the truck rode smoothly for its kind, and he was settling down as the city left them, averting his face from the blast of cold air that spilled over the front, taking shallow breaths and thinking that Canada had a big tourist problem if it was like this every June.

Then Requin left the main road, and he revised his opinion of the ride.

An hour later, or maybe it was six or seven years, he reached up to bang on the rear window and signal his surrender, offer a plea to be let in—god, he could sit on someone's lap. As he lifted himself to do it, however, he took note of the countryside and realized they were bouncing over the grassy perimeter of an old airfield dimly aglow with a few lights on high poles irregularly placed. He dropped down again. He told himself this was only a stop for gasoline, and Requin had his aircraft somewhere else, somewhere more civilized. He looked up again and didn't even see a tower.

Then Requin braked sharply in front of a hangar and was out on the ground before the engine stopped turning.

"Well," he said with a flourish of both arms, "all aboard what's getting aboard."

The twin-engine Cessna seated six behind the pilot, and with Alice up next to Pierre, there was plenty of room in back for Lincoln to find a seat to avoid looking out the disturbingly small windows. Unfortunately, he couldn't find one and was relegated to the one nearest the tail, not wanting to sit anywhere near the door. Annabelle professed not to be bothered by the size of the sleek craft, but Lincoln expressed the opinion loudly that he much preferred to have a bit more solid metal between him and the drop outside.

Requin told him, kindly, to stop bothering the pilot and stick to his sewing.

Lincoln did. Getting his friend piqued was the one thing, right now, he didn't want to do.

As it was, he figured they were in trouble not only with the Mantos, but with all the provincial and federal government offices that controlled air traffic within a radius of a thousand miles.

It was bad enough they were in a plane this small, but they had also taxied out to a ridiculously short runway in complete darkness, had taken off without Requin filing a flight plan or bothering to check with the airport manager (who, he said, was ten miles away in his farmhouse, probably drunk with his wife, and what he didn't know wouldn't hurt them, so why bother, eh?), and were now flying as low as the old man thought was safe, considering the time and the lay of the land.

That, Lincoln thought, was not safe enough.

With the moon providing them with the only light, he could see that they couldn't have been more than fifty feet above the tops of the trees that were, in themselves, incredibly tall, comprising a forest that stretched uninterrupted and black to the horizon—a horizon increasingly broken up by a series of ranges whose height he didn't want to even begin to guess.

Annabelle, whose experience in airplanes had obviously been restricted to commercial flight, was amazed.

Lincoln was too, but for much different reasons.

The Cessna climbed, banked, and off to the right he could see the moon-caught waters of Lesser Slave Lake, a lake large enough to be dubbed a small inland sea. It was beautiful, and for a moment he forgot about the ground dropping away below him and concentrated on the view, on the patches of snow still trapped in shadows, on the lakes, on the ridges, on the infrequent clutches of lights that marked the smaller towns.

He could see no roads.

There were no other planes in the sky.

Alice and Pierre were conferring about something, gesturing at the instruments and jabbing fingers at the stars, but the drone of the engines prevented his eavesdropping. He glanced to his left and saw Annabelle curled up in her seat, peacefully sleeping with her jacket for a pillow. He smiled. Looked out again, and soon found himself drifting off and not wanting to fight it.

He had no idea how long he'd slept, but the whine of the engines beginning a descent woke him with a start. It was still dark when he checked the window, so dark he couldn't see a sign of the runway. Annabelle slept on. Pierre was leaning forward in his seat, nodding and muttering to Old Alice, who was holding on to her sombrero.

The moon was gone.

The forest—or a plain; he was unable to tell which because the light was too dim and his eyes were too bleary—was still completely black, and he was pleasantly astonished when the wheels touched solid ground.

They taxied to an unlighted hangar, stopped, and Pierre motioned him silently to remain where he was. When Alice looked around at him with a question, he told her with a look not to ask it but to assume the old pilot was probably breaking the law and the less they knew about it the better.

In fifteen minutes they were airborne again, after a refueling that must, he figured, have set a world record.

They swung northward, and the elegant and low Birch Hills passed beneath them; northward again, and the small town of Fairview slipped behind with a whisper.

It was colder in the cabin now, much colder, and he was about to dredge out a blanket and bundle himself up when Requin landed again, just before dawn, in a field that was little more than grass and a tin shack with a fuel pump in front.

No one came out to greet them; as far as he could tell, there wasn't a road within twenty miles of the place.

"Don't get my sleep, I be walking soon," the pilot said when Lincoln asked him what was going on. He pointed to the sky growing light in the east. "Give me two, three hours, I'm right as rain, you don't worry."

Lincoln wasn't worried. What bothered him was the fact that

sooner or later either Annabelle or Alice was going to ask him about that three-leg journey they were supposed to take; and he was going to have to tell them it was more like ten or twelve, not because of the Cessna's range, but because they were taking a deliberately circuitous route in order, he hoped, to avoid detection.

Annabelle asked first; when he explained, she groaned and started hunting for a bathroom.

When he explained it to Alice, she hit him with a grape.

When Requin returned, Lincoln took him to one side and the pilot spread a map on the ground. It didn't take them long to decide that flying over British Columbia and then swinging north was probably the safest route to the Yukon since there were more places to put down in case there was trouble, and more airfields, such as they were, to pick up needed fuel. On the other hand, continuing up into the District of Mackenzie, the Northwest Territories, would provide them with more cover than they would probably need.

More cover, less help, and no guarantee they wouldn't run into a summer storm.

"Big bangs," Pierre said glumly, refolding the map. "Heavy wind, lousy rain, can't see worth a damn if we get caught in one. Take this old bird and slam her to the ground."

"Do you have parachutes?"

"Sure I do," he said, insulted Lincoln should ask. "One for me, one for the old lady. You know how to fly?"

"A plane?"

Requin flapped his arms.

"Wonderful."

Requin put an arm around his shoulders and walked him back to the aircraft. "I do the best I can, Linc, you know this. We did not have all the time I want to get ready."

"If we have to jump," he said, his stomach suddenly queasy, "can one of those things hold two people?"

The pilot laughed and shoved him inside. "You watch too many movies, Linc. By damn, too many movies."

They flew north.

By the end of their third day, cramped and irritable and praying it would all stop before they were permanently deformed, Requin landed neatly at a field just beyond Trout Lake, at the base of the Mackenzie Mountains. There was a Quonset hut at the far end of the runway, a smaller shack made of untrimmed logs midway along, and as they taxied slowly toward the fuel-staging area, Lincoln noticed again the lack of a committee to greet them.

Pierre noticed it too, and when he finally cut the engines and set the brakes, he held up a hand to keep them inside.

"I think," he said, "there is nobody here."

"Should there be?" Annabelle asked as she struggled into her jacket.

"Three, four. I know these people. The man is a Sioux who didn't follow Sitting Bull back. Smart. He found gold instead, and makes investments in New York."

Lincoln patted his side, where his revolver nested in his waistband, and pushed open the door, climbed out, and turned to help Annabelle down. Alice and the pilot were soon beside them, and they walked slowly toward the cabin, chatting, stretching, and watching the two windows that flanked the closed door.

"No dog," Requin muttered. "Big sucker. Part wolf."

The seemingly endless forest hemmed in the field and climbed the slopes to the peaks in the west. The air chilled, almost cold, despite the time of year, and there were still patches of snow and ice on the ground where the sun seldom reached them. A flock of geese flew over. The Cessna's engines cooled loudly. Lincoln pushed aside his jacket and covered the gun with his hand.

Requin called then, hands cupped around his mouth.

There was no answer, and the dog didn't bark.

"Pierre, take the ladies back to the plane and get the fuel you need. I think we're going to have to leave in a hurry."

Annabelle argued halfheartedly, but went along while Lincoln strode up to the door, knocked, and waited.

There was no answer, and the dog still didn't bark.

He tried the knob, and it turned, and he pushed the door open without stepping over the threshold.

The silence inside was too deep, too complete, and he only had to take a single pace in to see that no one was there, and no one was likely to return for a good long while.

The only thing he touched was on a table in the center of the front room—an ashtray with a cigar in it, and the cigar was still warm.

Well, he thought, don't that beat all.

And he was halfway back to the plane when he heard the growling in the forest, whirled, and saw a break of camouflage fall away and another plane roll out into the open.

He ran, shouting, and nearly threw himself to the ground when a cannon exploded and deafened him for a while. He whirled to answer fire, saw the plane still coming at him, and whirled again, this time to see Old Alice on one knee, her left hand holding up the sombrero's brim while the right fired the magnum again and the others leapt for the doors.

He scrambled in just behind them, just as Pierre fired the engines and started for the runway. The second plane followed at a reasonable distance, and Lincoln was puzzled until he realized they weren't trying to stop them. Before he could warn Requin, the Cessna was in the air, and their pursuers behind them, five miles back.

The Mackenzie Mountains loomed, rugged above the treeline, and capped with blinding snow.

Requin stayed as low as he could, flinging the plane and passengers through narrow passes that almost chopped off the wings, skirting lakes, topping trees, finally soaring over a plateau gold with summer grass.

Then the second plane closed, and Lincoln ducked instinctively as it roared overhead, banked sharply, and dove to climb behind them again. A second time made the Cessna drop a hundred feet in less than a second, made Annabelle whimper, and Alice took out her gun again. Lincoln only reached for the parachutes under the seat. Then he closed his eyes tightly when the Cherokee came so close Requin had to dive to avoid collision.

And kept on diving while he yelled, "Linc, my friend, I think we're going to crash."

TWENTY

Damn, I knew it, Lincoln thought as the old man struggled to bring the nose up; I knew I should have taken the bus.

The Cherokee buzzed them one more time, actually touching wingtips and sending the Cessna into a desperate screaming roll. The knapsacks flew around the cabin like stones, Lincoln saw the sky for a moment, the ground again, the sky a second time before Requin was able to pull them out, the veins on the sides of his neck so infused they were purple, so bloated they seemed like serpents under his skin.

"I gonna sue that bastard!" Pierre yelled. "He gonna help me retire, the forsuredamn Sunday driver!"

But the Cherokee was gone.

The angle of the dive eased, but they were still going down, and Lincoln pulled and clawed his way to the front, to whisper something in the man's ear.

Pierre shook his head violently and pointed at the meadow they were going to plow.

Lincoln insisted.

Pierre refused.

Lincoln suggested that time didn't permit much debate.

"You crazy?"

"You want to be sure we get killed?"

"We gonna die anyway, I think."

"Trust me," he said, and threw himself into the nearest seat, wrapped on the belt, and waited for a decision.

Requin couldn't look around to see the expression on Lincoln's face, but he did take one brief second to reach out and pat Alice's leg before he tried one last time to take the Cessna back into the air where she belonged. It shuddered, wavered side to side, and came around in a slow banking curve that had them thinking they had made it. But it only momentarily faced east before swinging back again, stubborn in its insistence that it wanted to land. He tried again, and when he failed, he shook his head, fought to straighten the aircraft out, then snapped out a hand toward the instrument panel.

The silence was terrifying when the engines cut out and the plane became a glider, more so because all Lincoln could hear was the scream of the wind, the pilot's frantic grunting as he sought to glide the plane in, and his own harsh breathing. Annabelle had dropped to the floor between seats and had curled up as tightly as she could; Alice was holding on to the seatbelt and swearing as the ground below lost its detail, blurring into currents of a brown-gold river whose banks just ahead rose into the wall of a forest.

The plane shuddered when Requin stiffened his arms; the passengers grabbed for anything they could find and held on when the wheels slammed once into the thick grass and bounced them fifty feet back into the air.

The trees neared.

The plane slammed down again, and Lincoln closed his eyes, covered his head when a horrid stench ripped through the cabin as the struts were wrenched off and the plane began an uncontrollable slide on its belly.

The trees came nearer still, and Requin gave a last shout before the plane slewed around and disintegrated into thunder.

The second Lincoln realized he wasn't dead, that they were on the ground and he was still breathing, he yanked off his seatbelt and charged for the door. The stench of fumes filled the cabin, and he knew it was only a matter of moments before the flames he saw snapping out of the engines on both crumpled wings blew the plane up. Requin was groaning in his seat, but Alice was already trying to pull him out. Annabelle had uncurled herself, and when Lincoln kicked the door free, she tossed out the knapsacks and scrambled after them in a hurry.

Smoke fogged the cabin.

Lincoln helped Alice with the old man, put him over his shoulder, and the three ran for the open meadow. They had slammed backward into the first line of trees, and several had been split in half by the force of the blow.

When they were less than fifty yards away, Lincoln unloaded the pilot and dove for the grass as the airplane exploded. Heat and sound blasted across the meadow, and they were pelted with smoking fragments of leather, metal, and wood. When he rolled onto his back, he saw a lazy pillar of ugly black smoke lifting into the sky. And a minute later the air was still; a minute after that he could hear birds singing in the forest, could hear the wind soughing in the branches, could hear off to his right the splash of a waterfall into a stream.

He sat up, hooked his hands around his knees, and looked down at Requin, who was sprawled on his back, holding his fur hat in both hands and gently patting out the fire. Old Alice was straightening her sombrero and blowing ashes off the grapes; and Annabelle was on her hands and knees, glaring at the wreckage as if daring it to blow up again.

"Well," he said.

They were lucky, and he knew it, and aside from assorted bruises and minor scratches, they were unharmed. But the reaction had already set in, and none of them spoke for a very long time.

And when they finally did, that too was part of the reaction. They babbled, they complained, they thanked every pantheon in the world for bringing them through; they compared injuries and exaggerated, they compared their last thoughts, and it was Requin who started them on a prolonged and cathartic spate of laughing.

Finally, seeing the sun nearing its zenith, Lincoln had them examine their packs to see what had been lost. The result was gratifying—their clothes were in fair shape, the first-aid kit was intact, and if they were within five blocks of a good grocery they wouldn't have to starve.

"Berries and bark," said Old Alice, getting to her feet and shouldering the knapsack. "Pioneers did it, so can we. It's good for the digestion. Keeps the bowels young."

Requin seemed skeptical and made an unpleasant noise with his tongue and his teeth, but Lincoln only stood with his hands on his hips and looked thoughtfully around him—at the rim of mountains that had created the shallow bowl for this meadow, at the height of the peaks and their June-caps of snow, at the absence of passes that trapped them in here. From a quick-fading memory of the map, now burned to cinders with the rest of the directional equipment, he estimated glumly they had just crossed into the Yukon, somewhere in the middle slopes of the Mackenzies. A gloomy confirmation from Requin pleased him, but he wasn't too happy about an added comment to the effect that they were still several hundred miles from Whitehorse without any way to get there.

And though the Cherokee hadn't returned, he could not give them assurance that it wouldn't, given time. Sooner or later, someone would want to know who, if anyone, had survived the wreck.

On the other hand, any survivors in country like this weren't much of a threat.

"I wish," he said aloud to no one in particular, "I knew exactly where we were."

For an answer, Old Alice smacked her lips, hitched up her rhinestone rattlesnake-skin belt, and stuck a finger in her mouth. Took it out a second later and held it up over her head as she turned slowly in a circle.

"My guess is Howatoon."

Annabelle giggled, and Requin clapped on his smoldering, woebegone fur hat, muttered something about senility in women with sombreros, and began making plans to carve his will on a tree. Lincoln, however, had been around the old woman too long to question her about matters of place. He didn't know how she did it, but when she did it, it was right.

"Which way," he asked, ignoring the others' protests of his supreme gullibility.

"That way," Alice told him, and pointed hard to the west.

"In that case," he said with a swift check of the sky, "I suggest we get moving before that dive bomber comes back."

He started off confidently, following Alice and listening to her explain about the various kinds of trees they were soon passing under—many of them firs twice as high as a house—the sparse underbrush, the identifications of the animal sounds they were hearing, though nothing showed itself save for a rustling in the shadows. Requin trailed, shaking his head and wondering at the top of his voice if he would ever see his beloved Edmonton again. Only Annabelle was silent, and Lincoln turned several times to see if she was hiding an injury worse than she'd admit; but she wouldn't meet his gaze, and wouldn't answer his questions, and he finally gave up to concentrate on their walk.

There was no trail to follow, but Alice seemed to know where she was going. They skirted huge boulders, some as wide as a cabin and just as tall; they forded a number of narrow streams whose water was cold enough to turn their skin a burned red just from the touching; they came upon the waterfall he had heard after the crash, a hundred-foot drop from a gap in slick rocks, resulting in a large pool from which they drank eagerly, and a rainbow-pierced mist that made him feel as though it were raining without clouds.

The direction was downward, the incline gentle enough to keep them from slipping though they had nothing to follow but faint deer trails and breaks between the shrubs; but when they reached a small clearing and he was able to look farther than the nearest tree trunk, he began to have his doubts.

Below them was a huge oval valley several miles wide, more mountains beyond, and the only thing he could see was the forest sweeping on. There were no signs he could detect of human habitation; there were no signs of logging, roads, or attempts at mining.

There were no signs of anything but a heaven for squirrels.

Requin took the pause to mean a break, and promptly dropped to the ground. He pulled off his boots and massaged his feet, took off his hat and woefully examined the damage the explosion had done. Annabelle sat beside him, staring absently at the evergreens and at the high, flat-bottomed clouds drifting down from the north.

Lincoln squatted then and waited until Alice had sat alongside him Indian-fashion. With a twig he dug at the ground, played cricket with a pebble, and absently began drawing what resembled a map.

"Alice?"

She lit a cigarette and blew smokerings toward the clouds.

"Alice, do you have any idea where we are?"

"I already told you," she said petulantly.

"I know, I know. Howatoon." He looked over the valley and pointed. "So where is it?"

"Down there."

"Down there is trees."

"Under the trees."

"You mean, underground?"

"No, I mean under the trees. Low buildings, you can't see them from here."

He glanced at her sideways. "Alice, who the hell are you kidding?"

She stubbed the cigarette out, took his twig, and dug it a grave. When she was positive there was no chance of a fire starting in the bed of browned needles carpeting the forest floor, she broke the twig in half and tossed it over her shoulder.

"Howatoon," she said, "is short for Howard's Town. Some kind of funny accent the man had, something like that. Howard, Mr. Know-It-All Tailor—and I don't recollect his last name, so don't ask —was a miner looking for the mother lode and didn't want to be with the rest of the idiots who were digging in the snow north of here. So he strikes out on his own and gets himself lost before he can think twice about turning around. But he was an old fart so he didn't know anything, and he liked it, and he didn't want to ruin the landscape, so to speak, so he made sure that the house he built never showed."

"Sounds to me like he didn't want anyone to find him."

"That too."

"Why?"

"Killed a man."

"Ah."

"Found himself with some company a bit later, and a few more straggled in, and the next thing he knew, he had himself an empire."

"Some empire."

"Some people don't think as big as other people."

He shifted, plucked at the needles, dumped them from palm to palm as though he were casting runes. "So Howatoon is down there.

Founded by a murderer, and, I suppose, that so-called company included a few who didn't care if the Mounties never saw them again."

She nodded.

"That's wonderful, Alice. That's . . . wonderful."

"Thought you'd like it."

He sniffed, rubbed a hand over his face, and lifted the brim of her sombrero so he could see her face. "I suppose that means the Mantos are, too."

She nodded.

He released the hat and clucked to himself. Then he turned on the flats of his soles and faced the others. After outlining the story he'd just heard, he told them they would have to be more circumspect in their approach. He didn't think it would do to run smack into the middle of the town square while Storm and Rain were hanging around.

"How do you know they're here?" Annabelle asked tonelessly.

He didn't realize it until now, but it was unnervingly true when he said, "I can feel it."

She closed one eye and stared at him, turned away, and walked back into the trees.

Alice sighed. "Still can't get over her father doing that, can she?"

"No," he said.

Requin sat up. "Father?"

"I'll explain later," he said. "Right now we've got to get closer, so I can see this place. We have to have a plan, or we're going to get me killed."

Annabelle came back out of the trees.

"What do you mean, 'me'?" Alice said. "Don't the rest of us count?"

Lincoln gave her a smile that made her shudder.

Annabelle shuffled closer.

"Now look," he said, "we should eat now, get some water, and get moving. We have to have a place to hide before it gets dark. And we still don't have a plan."

"I do," Annabelle said.

"What?"

"You can start by running."

And she collapsed on the ground, with an arrow in her back.

TWENTY-ONE

Old Alice and Requin were instantly on their feet with muttered expressions of surprise and disgust, but Lincoln dropped without thinking beside the prone Annabelle, one trembling hand on her shoulder while he reached blindly for the gun he had tucked into his waistband. As his fingers moved to search for the woman's pulse, he scanned the heavy trees to the west for signs of the attacker. But there was no one there that he could see, nothing that he could find out just by looking. Then he heard a twig snap behind him and he whirled, stopping just short of pulling the weapon out.

"Good move, tailor, you get to live," said a quietly gloating Storm Manto, gliding blackly out of the shadows. He was holding a large, elaborately balanced bow, with a hunting arrow already nocked and aiming.

"Very good move," said a second voice.

He whirled again in a crouch, frustration at his lack of caution making him groan, and Rain was coming up behind them, with a hunting bow as well, and a gold-tipped arrow pointed straight at Old Alice's chest.

The brothers were still wearing their cowboy clothes, and here in the forest they looked more like animated skeletons than ever. It chilled him and made him wish he'd taken up insurance instead of tailoring.

"Maybe," said a third, deeper voice, and Lincoln decided to stop counting all the delightful surprises when Peter Wolf moved in from the left, a more conventional revolver in his hand. He wore a dark sheepskin-and-leather jacket, and his elkskin trousers were fringed. "It depends on whether you want to die now or later." His smile was void of humor. "I would suggest now, all things considered."

As slowly as he could, Lincoln pulled his gun out, considered the odds and found them lousy, even for Superman. So he flipped the gun over, held it by the barrel and threw it on the ground at Storm's feet. Requin stiffened and muttered to himself, then reached into his hat, pulled out the sweatband and exposed a derringer he kissed once and tossed away. Alice did nothing but pull her sequined purse to her scrawny chest and act the prim and shocked old woman.

Then Annabelle moaned and tried to push herself up. Lincoln said, "Take it easy, don't move," and ignored the others to check on the extent of her wound. A wound, he finally saw with a great sigh of relief, extended no farther than the bulging knapsack whose contents had taken and absorbed the blow of the arrow. Her jacket wasn't even nicked, though he suspected she wouldn't be walking completely upright for a while.

When he looked to Storm for permission and received it with a curt nod, he yanked the arrow out, broke it in half, and dropped it; then he stripped off the knapsack, took her arms, and pulled her gently to her feet. Her eyes were glazed from the force of the blow, but they cleared quickly, and she scowled when she saw the predicament they were in.

"Didn't I tell you once you were no fun, Lincoln," she said, trying to reach behind her to rub at the bruise on her spine.

"At least," he said, "you're not dead."

"Yeah," she said sourly, and her face darkened when she saw her father. A murderous lunge at the Indian's throat was aborted only when Linc tightened his grip, cautioning her with hasty whispers about the difference between a short and a long life. She didn't believe him. It was obvious she was ready to try again, and he yanked her around and glared into her eyes until she could no longer meet his gaze.

"All right," she said reluctantly. "But I'm not making any promises."

He nodded: *Fair enough.*

"You two finished?" Storm asked.

"What are my choices?"

The bow and arrow lifted, making a target of the middle of his brow.

"Fair enough," he said.

Quickly then, and staying well back from any foolhardy attempt at heroics, the Mantos and Wolf picked up their weapons. After a brief, unintelligible conference during which Rain started to pout and Wolf punched him hard on the arm, they herded them into the forest, down into the Howatoon Valley. They said nothing beyond a few directional grunts, and all three remained spread well apart behind. When Old Alice slipped on a moss-covered rock, no one moved to help her. When Requin took off his hat again, an arrow bit it from his hand and pinned it to a bole; he didn't try to retrieve it.

The shadows deepened as the trees grew closer together, and the temperature began to fall as the sun slipped lower in the sky.

Lincoln fastened his jacket, letting his hand slide once and with relief over the bulge in his shirt pocket. The relief, however, was not as complete as he'd like when he recalled all the knocks and bumps, including the plane crash, the vial had taken. If it hadn't gone off then, he couldn't be sure it would go off when he needed it.

Palmer, he thought, needs to practice some more.

An hour later they reached the bottom of the slope, and Storm went ahead to pull away what looked like an impassable barrier of thorn bushes. They were, in fact, little more than branches thrown together and, once gone, revealed a clear and worn trail that led toward the valley's center.

"The yellow brick road," Linc said with a grin to Rain. "Which one are you, the scarecrow?"

The White Rider laughed, and he decided never to try a joke on them again—the laugh was high, rattling, and carried into the dark foliage like a carrion crow.

Storm shifted aside and gestured them to move on. Requin, peering into the brush and up into the branches, shook his head stubbornly. He didn't like not being able to see places large enough to land or fly a plane. Old Alice moved to him then and took his elbow, urging him silently until he finally agreed, though he never stopped looking up, his head cocked to one side as though listening for an engine.

Annabelle walked beside Lincoln, and he could see that dark, pensive expression on her face again. He touched her back once, and she shrugged him away.

"It's hard, I know," he said, hoping to be of some comfort.

"You don't know the half of it," she growled.

Rain ordered them to be quiet and was angrily overruled by Storm. Wolf was nowhere to be seen, but Linc never doubted the man had them all in his sights.

Another hour passed, and he wondered if someone had switched calendars on him; the darkening twilight in the forest was too much like winter, and he imagined that temperatures in December, up here in the north, weren't exactly like those he was used to in New Jersey. And when the wind began to blow, howling through the boughs and keening high on the peaks, he decided Santa Claus was a jerk for not operating out of Venezuela.

The trail widened, and others crossed or melded into it from other directions.

Once, Storm ordered them to halt when they heard a violent thrashing deep to their left. Linc didn't want to know what it was, but Storm told him anyway: "Grizzly. We'll wait a bit, see where he's going."

"Thanks," he said.

"No problem." Manto grinned. "I have to be sure you get there in one piece."

"Then why'd you crash my baby!" Requin demanded, only just stopping short of charging the man.

"You would've passed over and kept on going," the White Rider explained, cutting in on his brother.

"We could've been killed!"

Storm shook his head. "I know you, old man. You wouldn't have crashed. I just forced you down."

"That's true," Requin said with a smug grin. "I pretty good, now you mention it."

"But not immortal," Manto reminded him.

"Hell, no one lives forever."

Manto frowned, and Linc was once again struck how the cunning the Mantos had could be coupled with such monumental denseness. It must, he decided, run in the family.

The thrashing faded in the opposite direction, and they moved on. The trail widened even further. The trees began to pull away from each other, and the underbrush had evidently been cleared by hand. To his left he caught a glimpse of a building, and he nodded to himself, remembering Old Alice's story—from the brief look he could see it was only one story and built in such a small clearing that the trees came right up to its walls, the branches laced overhead to hide it from inspection from the sky.

A mental apology to Alice, then: on his own, he never would have found this place. Never in a million years.

Then he frowned. Scowled. Stopped suddenly in his tracks and nearly pulled Annabelle off her feet.

"What now?" she said.

" 'What now,' you ask?"

He spun on Requin, who inhaled deeply and said, "Oops."

Lincoln nodded. Alice may have known where Howatoon was, but Lincoln had specifically ordered the pilot to make the trip as long and complicated as possible. Only someone directly on their tail the entire way could have traced them—or someone who had been told of the itinerary once it started. As probably happened during their first stop, when Requin had vanished for a while and had returned without explanation.

"Goddamnit, Pierre, you owed me one!"

Requin shrugged. "You say it was nothing. I took you at your word."

"So you double-crossed me, all this was an act?"

The pilot spread his hands, thumping Old Alice on the chest and staggering her backward. "I am not a young man. I need a pension."

"Jesus," he grumbled. "Then the plane wasn't going to crash."

Requin shook one hand side to side. "It wasn't supposed to. I was carried away." His grin was broad. "I am an actor, too, you see. Many years ago."

"You were carried away," he said sourly.

"The heat of the moment."

"Yeah." He turned and walked on, ignoring the idiotic grins on the faces of the Mantos. "Damn, now what?"

"You really want to know?" Annabelle said.

He stopped again, not sure he could take it. "What?" he said cautiously. "Are you one of them, too?"

"Hey, tailor, watch your mouth!"

"All right, then . . ." He put his hands on his hips, and waited patiently. There was no hurry. Whatever she told him couldn't make the situation worse.

"Peter Wolf."

He leaned forward slightly. "Yes?"

"His name is only sort of Wolf."

His mouth opened a little.

"He isn't my father."

A little more.

"He's a Canadian Sioux."

Lincoln wanted to sit down.

"Wolf is his Indian name."

"You're killing me."

"His Anglo name is Manto."

TWENTY-TWO

They left the main trail for one more narrow, and soon reached a cabin Lincoln knew he did not want to enter. From the outside it looked to be no more than a single room with a roof and a chimney, but he had been struck by the way the trees and brush had been cleared around it and the one he had seen earlier, and after a quick scan of the area he nodded—between two man-sized boulders he could see the pointed cap of a stove's chimney. There were rooms underground then, and there was no telling how many.

Rain gestured with his bow and the three of them sat while Requin and Storm went inside. Then he positioned himself by the door and leaned back. Smiling.

Old Alice pushed back the sombrero and sighed loudly. "I misjudged him," she said bitterly. "Just goes to show you should never trust an old fart."

Lincoln, however, put a hand on Annabelle's shoulder, squeezing it until she looked at him and saw the query in his eyes. She was reluctant, and obviously a little afraid, but he was neither angry nor disappointed, only resigned.

When she spoke, he had to lean forward to hear her, though he never once took his eyes off Rain and his bow.

The story she had told him of her mother's affair with an Indian was true, but the man was Navajo and died shortly after Mrs. Bannon did, in an automobile accident. Peter Wolf showed up at the ranch looking for work. Annabelle had taken a liking to him, hired him without bothering to ask for references, and was soon dependent on him and his handling of the hands. He was friendly, but discouraged friendship, and it wasn't long before she found herself falling in love with him. Working with him daily, then, became agony, and though she knew she was being foolish, she could not help herself. At one point, she said, she nearly threw herself at him in a vain attempt at seduction. The seduction failed. Peter Wolf changed.

One week later he came unbidden into her bedroom. She thought this might be it, all her plans come to fruition. She changed her mind when she saw the gun in his hand, knew she was wrong when he proceeded methodically to whip her with a lariat, then tied her to the bedpost. He explained very carefully that he had some business to do with her uncle, that she was to play her part better than she had done with him, and if she didn't, she would be the first to know that Farren Upshire was dead. He also threatened some rather unspeakable, if intriguing, practices on her own body should she attempt to interfere.

Then he called Farren, not the other way around—after, not before, he'd found the Konochine Pueblo. It seemed that Knight was known to the Mantos long before Upshire heard of it.

Lincoln listened without comment until she was done, then hugged her once around the shoulders in an effort to tell her he was used to this sort of thing, don't worry. She didn't smile.

"What I don't get is," he said at last, "why you didn't say something at the airport."

A deep breath gave her time to meet his gaze. "The people who worked for me, Lincoln, had been on that land for a lot longer than the Bannons. I owed them. They would have died if I'd said anything."

"They did anyway," he said sadly, and told her about the graves he'd discovered on the hill.

"I . . ." She wiped a hand over her face, back through her hair. "I guess I knew that. I just didn't want to." A wan smile, and she looked at him again. "Besides, I didn't know you. I mean, Loraleen tells me that Uncle is sending out a tailor to take care of things, and what am I supposed to believe?"

"I understand."

"I mean, a tailor, for crying out loud!"

"Okay, okay."

"What I'm saying is . . . a tailor?"

"All right, all right, I get the picture."

"Honest to god," she said. "At least a butcher carries a knife, you know what I mean?"

She grabbed his arm then, and her eyes suddenly opened wide, her gaze drifting slowly from his face down his arm to where her grip encircled the sheath under his sleeve.

"Oh."

He nodded. "Now I know I can count on you not to betray us tailors, right?"

She nodded this time.

"And you'll hold off trying to get your uncle's land until after we get out of here?"

"Sure."

"Good girl."

Old Alice jabbed him in the ribs with an elbow. "Dem bones are coming back."

He looked up just as the door opened and Storm stepped out. A deep breath, and he scowled, muttered something to Rain, who pushed away from the cabin and strolled over to them. He said not a word, but gestured them curtly to their feet, stood aside, and followed them to the door. Storm backed away. Lincoln felt Annabelle grab his hand, and he stepped over the threshold.

He was right.

The room inside was practically devoid of furniture. There was a mock fireplace on the back wall, a chair beside the hearth, and nothing else by the bare, unfinished walls. In the center of the floor, however, was a large opening framed by a railing on three sides; on the open side he could see steps leading down, and when the door was slammed and bolted behind him, he didn't need further direction. With Annabelle ahead and Alice behind, he started down, and found himself in a room twice as large as the one above.

Here the walls were made of smooth, brown stone flecked through with glints of gold, and covered here and there with treated hides of polar bear, grizzly, walrus, and shark. The stairwell was on the back wall, flanked by massive oak wardrobes whose doors were securely padlocked. The floor was carpeted, and in its center was an island of sturdy, handmade furniture positioned around a five-foot-wide coffee table made from a section of pine. Oil lamps hung from the ceiling on braided chains, and on the endtables beside each chair were curiously old-fashioned lamps of milky white, with tasseled shades.

The resulting light took the sharp edges from the wood, made the stone seem much softer, made the hides seem almost as if they were painted on the walls.

"Cozy," he said, and was prodded from behind toward the nearest chair. He considered resisting, then changed his mind. Now that he was here, he needed to know exactly what was going on. Storm and Rain had given him hints, but he wasn't about to take any of them literally until he could see for himself what their plan was. After that he would play it by ear.

Once they were settled, Requin headed for the middle of three doors in the back wall. With a look over his shoulder he disappeared through it, and Lincoln wasn't quick enough to see what lay beyond. Then he settled back, smiling blandly as Rain fetched a tray of glasses from a wet bar he didn't see when he'd come down. The tray was placed on the pine table. Alice sniffed at it as if insulted, but he shrugged, reached out, and took up a glass.

"Don't," Annabelle warned hastily. "It might be poison or something."

"No," he reassured her. "Poison isn't what's happening here. I suggest you drink up. The most that can happen," he said as she put the glass to her lips, "is that you'll be drugged."

She spit the liquid out and wiped her mouth.

Old Alice sniffed again, then emptied her own glass in a single gulp, held it up and over her shoulder until Rain filled it again from a dark red decanter. She didn't thank him. He stuck out his tongue.

Lincoln sipped once and grimaced. It was a Canadian wine better suited to luring whales and wolves to destruction than to human consumption. He placed the glass back on the table and folded his hands over his stomach.

"Well, here we are."

Storm waited until Rain had left the room through the lefthand door, then took a chair himself, his bow exchanged for a loaded rifle. "You won't have long to wait, tailor," he said without expression.

"I assume all this nonsense has something to do with Knight's tail?"

Manto shifted uncomfortably before he nodded. "Sooner or later."

"I suppose you wouldn't like to explain?"

Manto caressed the rifle's barrel thoughtfully. "I'm not supposed to."

"I thought you were in charge?" he asked innocently.

"I am!"

"Then if you're in charge, who can tell you what to do and what not to do?"

"Me," said Peter Wolf as he came down the stairs. "Storm is a lot of things, a lot of good things, but being in charge isn't one of them."

Storm half rose, and sank again when Wolf gave him a simple look. He held the look until he had circled his company, then transferred it to Annabelle, who was gripping the arms of her chair as if bracing herself for a launch.

"No," he cautioned.

She relaxed, but only slightly.

"So," Lincoln said, "your real name is Manto?"

"In a way," Wolf said, getting himself a drink and eyeing the doors. "Semirelated to Tremain, you could say."

"Semi?"

"My half brother," Wolf said.

Uh-oh, he thought.

"But that's not important," the Indian said airily, and resumed his circling of the room. "What is important is the fact that you are here, Mr. Blackthorne, at the request of the Manto family. I am sorry to have been so devious, but I had a feeling you wouldn't accept an ordinary invitation."

"You're right. And since it's me you're after—"

"Oh, for god's sake," Wolf said, annoyed. "Don't tell me you're going to say, 'Then let the women go and we can do our business man-to-man.' Because if you are," he continued before Lincoln could respond, "the answer is no."

"Damn," said Old Alice.

The center door opened, and Requin staggered out with a long box in his arms. He edged his way into the middle of the furniture island and placed it on the table. Storm raised the rifle. Wolf stood behind Lincoln's chair while Requin struggled with the lid.

"You see, Mr. Blackthorne, my brother and you were not the best of friends, as you recall. Subsequently, because of your last meeting, Tremain's mind went on a trip. All he thought about was getting revenge for what you had done to his face. He wanted to do terrible things to you, Mr. Blackthorne. Terrible things."

Lincoln watched as the traitorous pilot finally wrenched the lid off the box and dropped it on the floor. He could not see inside, but he knew what was there. Wolf came around him, then, and reached in and pulled out the tail.

"Well, well," said Old Alice. "So that's what all the fuss is about."

"Indeed, old woman," Wolf said without taking his eyes off Lincoln. "All the fuss. For all these years."

The gold shone brilliantly in the soft lamplight, and the rubies held tiny images of trapped and writhing fire. Wolf's face hardened. The tail began to spin. Alice and Annabelle looked away instinctively, but Lincoln refused; he knew—and realized he had known for some time—what the Mantos wanted it for.

And it wasn't for the fortune entwined in the hair.

"Ah, you understand," Wolf said, his lips pulled away from his teeth in a typical Manto grin.

"That's not what it's for," Lincoln said, his throat dry and feeling coated with sand.

"I know that. But it's worth a try, isn't it?"

"Know what?" Annabelle said.

Lincoln groaned silently.

"Well, my darling Annabelle," the Indian said, turning slowly, so slowly they hardly knew he had moved, "Tremain is dead. Several times over, as a matter of fact. This legendary amulet from far Arabia cures wounds and illness. And what, my dear, is a greater illness than death?"

"That's . . . that's . . ." She looked wildly around the room, searching for the word.

"Yes," Wolf said, "it is."

"But you don't even know it'll work!" she blurted.

Big mouth, Lincoln thought, and considered saying it aloud when hands reached over the back of his chair and yanked him to his feet. It was Rain. He hadn't seen the man enter the room, and though he managed to begin a valiant struggle, he was in no position to win when Requin joined Manto and they wrestled him to a thronelike chair against the opposite wall. On either side hung polar bear skins, and he examined them balefully while his wrists were tied to the armrests.

When the two were finished, he faced the room again and watched as Storm left his chair to stand beside Wolf. The rifle was at his shoulder.

Annabelle left her seat in a rush, but Requin was there before she could clear the island. He thrust her down again, and clamped a hand around her throat from behind, exerting just enough pressure to give her air to breathe, and precious little else. Alice reached up for a grape, and lowered her hand slowly when Rain tsked and showed her the knife he carried in his belt.

Then Wolf moved to one side.

"Don't worry, Mr. Blackthorne," he said, honestly smiling this time. "We don't intend to kill you."

"Thank you."

Storm pulled the trigger—three times.

The retort was deafening in the room, but Lincoln could only hear his own gasp as the bullets ripped through his jacket, his shirt, and buried themselves in his chest.

Skunked again, he thought, as Storm fired again.

The last thing he heard was Annabelle, screaming.

TWENTY-THREE

Being dead, he thought tranquilly, was actually not all that bad, all things considered, though he had rather enjoyed the alternative, even with Carmel and her damned marriage plans. A little on the chilly side, maybe, but not so terribly uncomfortable that he couldn't learn to get used to it in a century or two; and darker than he would have liked, though he was sure his eyes would soon adjust.

All in all, a rather comfortable feeling.

Until he tried to move in the unrelieved blackness and the fire rushed from the center of his chest to his ribs, his waist, down the length of his arms to his hands, which clenched so tightly cramps began spreading outward from the gaps between his knuckles. He wanted to scream, but he could produce no sound that he could hear; he wanted to cry, but his eyes felt too dry; he wanted to run from whatever came at him in the dark, but his legs were useless and he had to sit there, waiting, until another wave of cold washed over him, from his neck to his groin, up and down, until his teeth were chattering and his jaw and ears ached, and his lungs suddenly filled with a rush of melting ice.

On second thought, he decided, being dead wasn't fun.

"I don't believe it!"

"I don't believe it either, girl, but there you have it."

Angels should believe in everything, he thought; otherwise, it was blasphemy or something.

"It's a miracle!"

Of course it's a miracle. All life is a miracle. The miracle is that we know it's a miracle before we drop dead too soon to enjoy it.

That didn't make sense.

He opened his eyes and, after blinking at the lamplight that was for a moment too bright, found himself still sitting in the chair. His wrists were now unbound and, when he looked down, his jacket was off and his shirt filled with holes. In his lap lay the tail of the Arabian, Knight.

The gold glittered, the rubies winked, and it felt unnaturally cold.

"Well, I'll be damned," he said.

The others, the Mantos among them, watched openmouthed as he pulled aside the tattered remnants of his shirt to examine his skin. He knew at least three bullets had struck him—recalled with startling, horrid clarity the force and the pain, and gasped in the memory—yet there was no sign of entry anywhere. Not a scratch, not a bruise, not a single drop of blood. He pulled the skin, poked at it, looked up and grinned like a jerk.

"Blanks, right?"

Storm shook his head dumbly.

Lincoln blinked once, slowly, and passed out.

When consciousness returned, he was still in the chair, but now his wrists were rebound. His eyes opened before he could think, but the effort would have been wasted—he was alone, save for Old Alice, who was trussed and thrown on the sofa and glaring at him angrily.

"Where?" he demanded as quietly as he could and still be heard.

She squirmed to sit up, then nodded toward the three doors, nodded again toward the staircase and looked up at the ceiling.

He winked, though he didn't feel at all jaunty. What he felt was indescribable, and he hoped he'd have the time to think over what had happened. He didn't know if he had died, but it didn't matter; he was close enough to it, and after being brought back he didn't want ever to be that close again.

The Mantos, however, would have other ideas.

A prayer then to Palmer, and he worked his fingers until he was sure their reflexes were back. Then he sprang the knife from its sheath, caught it, and grinned as he deftly worked it around to cut through the rope. When the arm was free, he untied the other knot, hurried to Alice and parted the cord with a single slice.

The center door opened, and Requin stepped out.

"Hey, damnit!" he said.

"Damnit yourself, you old fart," Alice said.

Requin didn't know whether to charge the two escapees or rush back where he'd come from; and the hesitation was fatal.

Lincoln threw the knife, which buried itself high in the pilot's chest. Requin gasped and grabbed the hilt. Lincoln started for him to finish the job, but the old man's knees buckled and he fell flat on his face. The knife was driven deeper. He jumped once and was still.

With a motion to Alice to stay behind and watch the stairs, he darted inside and found himself in a deep clothes closet.

Out again, and in the righthand door.

Another room, this one slightly bigger and lined with shelves crammed with tins and sacks and jars topped with wax.

"Third time the charmer," he said to Old Alice, who was growing impatient.

The lefthand door gave easily onto a corridor that led gently downward. The only light came from the room behind, and his shadow started ahead of him, fading as he reached an abrupt turn to the left. There was no door in the gap he faced, and he could see without straining an all too familiar room.

The fire pit in the center, the caldron still hanging above it; oil lamps fixed to the stone walls, dust on the stone floor, and the three Mantos standing with their backs to him.

The lamps, however, had been extinguished; there was no need for them now. The only light came from the depths of the pit itself, crimson and wavering and casting shadows on the wall that made vision difficult. The heat, too, was intense, an almost tangible hellish creature that rose from the fire to fill the room with night.

Dropping to his hands and knees, Lincoln took a deep calming breath and entered, squinting into the flaring light for any clue he could find to Annabelle's whereabouts. He deliberately did not consider that they'd dropped her in the pit.

He hadn't gone more than a yard when he saw her lying in a heap against the wall. She was untied, but she was unconscious, and there was an ugly welt spreading on her temple, a slip of blood on her cheek.

He was about to crawl to her while the Mantos' attention was elsewhere, when as he moved he finally saw what they were looking at.

It was a crudely made wooden bier, its tall endposts nothing more than severed tree trunks still covered with bark, its platform four logs lashed together and covered by several layers of thick white hide.

And stretched out on the hide, the twisted, decomposing body of Tremain Manto.

The fire rose from the pit and licked red and gold at the scorched bottom of the caldron; heat rose in waves and ripples to cascade from the ceiling; the only sound was from the flames that crackled ten feet below the surface.

Peter Wolf was in the middle, and in his hands he held the amulet. He was muttering something and bobbing his head, and the brothers on either side were watching Tremain's sunken face with both fear and anticipation. Then the tail rose and fell and struck the corpse on the chest.

Annabelle stirred.

The tail rose and fell, its gold now more like bronze, its rubies more like blood.

The wall of flame suddenly flared upward in a deafening rush to engulf the caldron and send a billowing cloud of steam from whatever boiled inside.

Linc moved crabwise to the fallen woman and put a hand over her mouth just as her eyes fluttered. She looked up and started to struggle, saw who it was and relaxed. He could feel her lips smiling, and after a jerk of his head toward the men by the bier, he smiled in return and took his hand away.

"Goddamnit, Lincoln," she said loudly, "you didn't tell me about this!"

It wouldn't, he told himself, be the first time he'd killed a woman, but some innate goodness and a healthy fear of wasting time stopped him from throttling her. Instead, he jerked her to her feet and shoved her hard at the exit. At the same time, Storm and Rain turned around, saw him, and grinned.

The flames rose, and hissed.

The caldron rocked on its chain.

Peter Wolf dropped the tail onto the corpse's chest, its legs, its scarred and skull-like face.

Rain moved first, nodding as though he knew this would happen. Storm circled around to the side. Lincoln feinted toward the former, and lunged toward the latter, catching his chin with a blow that rocked him back against the bier.

Wolf didn't move.

The chest of the corpse began to rise and fall.

Rain threw an arm around his neck, and Linc dropped to one knee, straightened, and tossed the White Rider at his brother. The two men collided and fell in a tangle. They sorted themselves out quickly, Storm backpedaling to gain his balance while Rain pulled himself up by grabbing the bier.

Then he gaped at the breathing corpse.

Lincoln was too astonished to react; the White Rider suddenly bellowed in terror and bolted for the exit. Linc tried to stop him, but a shoulder caught him full in the chest, and he fell against the wall, too late to do anything but listen to the terrified man racing up the tunnel.

Storm, on the other hand, only tossed his black hat aside and came in for the kill.

Linc saw him more shadow than substance, and hurriedly shook off the effects of the stone colliding with his spine. He sidled away in a crouch, and they sparred warily for position, neither one connecting until Linc decided it was no fun being fair—he dropped to a knee, grabbed a handful of dust and tossed it in the man's face.

Storm glowered at the second time he'd been done by that trick, and Linc threw a punch that landed square on his cheek, staggering him back into the bier. He followed up swiftly and grabbed the man's throat, leaning him back over his dead father, feeling the searing heat from the pit begin to turn his face red. Storm aimed a knee at his groin, and he danced away, still holding the man's black shirt and pulling him back with him. Then he pushed and let go, and Storm's arms flailed, whacking Wolf on the shoulder and half turning him around.

Lincoln kicked the man's kneecap, and Storm fell back with a cry, grabbing desperately at the side of the bier to keep from tumbling into the fire. The bier turned on its blunted feet, Storm's hand slipped off, and all he could do was grin as he fell into the pit.

The flames exploded, the caldron rocked, and Peter Wolf drew the amulet over the dead man's lips.

The heat grew to a full-bore furnace, and Lincoln felt himself weakening, but he leapt on the Indian's back and pulled him away. Wolf spun with a snarl, his teeth bared as his hands reached for Linc's throat; Linc dodged and threw an uppercut that tripped the Indian backward. He yelled, and the tail dropped onto Tremain, smoking as the flames lowered below the pit's lip.

"You're too late," Wolf said. "You're too late, tailor."

The chest rose and fell, and the left hand began to tremble.

Wolf charged, and Lincoln was too slow—his head snapped back at a punch, again, and a third time when he was slammed against the wall. Trying to shake off the numbing effects of the stifling heat, his arms snared Wolf's to his side, and they stood there in the firelight, their shadows high on the wall, each trying to break the other's hold, kicking, grunting, finally dropping to their knees.

Tremain Manto sat up.

And screamed.

Lincoln and Wolf stopped their stalemated struggle long enough to stare incredulously at the thing on the bier. Then Wolf pushed him away and staggered to his feet, his mouth working, his head shaking side to side in terrified denial. Lincoln knew what he was thinking—the amulet worked, but it had only cured the death.

It had not cured the decomposition—it was too late for that.

Tremain Manto sat rigidly on the makeshift bier, large yellowed sections of his ribs and skull and femur exposed; his high, sloping forehead was pocked darkly with the bullet holes that had split it, and his lower jaw dangled open, the teeth black and stunted; most of his hair was gone, and what was left was smoldering from the heat of the pit; and when he turned to face them, they could see there was nothing in the eyesockets but fire-dancing shadows.

"Blackthorne," Tremain said, his voice filling the room. "Blackthorne, come here."

Wolf uttered a terrified cry and stumbled toward his brother, but

Lincoln jumped to his feet and pressed himself hard against the wall.

"Blackthorne, I want you!"

He swallowed against the bile spilling into his throat, then launched himself at Wolf's back, shoving and pushing as hard as he could until the Indian plunged forward, screaming, landing in his brother's embrace, the force of the collision toppling the bier.

For a moment nothing moved.

For a moment Lincoln only gaped.

Then Tremain bellowed, "I want you, Blackthorne," and their momentum carried them over the side.

TWENTY-FOUR

Lincoln staggered slowly out of the room, trying to wipe the perspiration from his face with a sleeve that was drenched with it, not all from the heat. The rough corridor upward seemed twice as long now as it had when he'd gone down, but the cooler the air grew, the more energy he felt, and when he at last staggered into the underground living room, he was smiling.

"Well," he said, "that takes care of that."

"Big deal," said the White Rider, and trained a rifle on his heart.

Lincoln ignored him. He was tired, he was aching, he was still trying to figure out how he was going to forget the voice that called his name from beyond the grave. What he didn't need now was some idiot giving orders from behind the safety of a rifled barrel.

He dropped into a chair, stretched out his legs, and sighed.

"Lincoln!"

Annabelle was standing against one of the wardrobes by the stairs, Old Alice beside her, tapping her foot with impatience.

"Ladies," he said, "I think we're captured."

"Damn right," said the White Rider. "Now you get your butt in gear and let's go."

"You're kidding. Where?"

Rain jerked the rifle up. "Come on, let's move it!"

"Not until I know where we're going."

"Lincoln," Annabelle warned. "He's got a gun."

"I can see that," he said testily. "And his brother, his uncle, and his old man are dead. One of them again. What's he going to do, call in his army?"

"Yeah," Rain said.

"No," Lincoln said. "Because if you had one, they would have been here from the start. Sorry, pal, but you're the last of the Mohicans."

"The last of the Mohicans still has a gun," Annabelle said.

"You don't have to keep reminding him of it."

Rain had had enough. He turned around and tightened his finger on the trigger. "The lady dies, tailor, unless you get to your feet."

Lincoln blew out a breath, and rose, and allowed himself and the others to be herded back up to the surface and out the door. Night had fallen, and there were only a few patches of moonlight on the ground to show them the way between the trees. His mind seemed numb, but he had pushed Manto as far as he could, and now he was forced to admit that he needed the man—to get them out of Howatoon unharmed, and back to civilization, or a reasonable facsimile thereof.

He was surprised, then, to realize they were heading back toward the meadow, less surprised when, a few hours later, they reached it and he saw an airplane standing in the tall grass. The Cherokee, and he could not immediately think of anything he'd rather see right now.

What he didn't count on was being required to fly it.

"Out of the question," he said.

"Yeah?" Manto replied.

"Yeah," he said. "I can't."

"What's the matter, you scared of heights?"

"Aside from that, I don't know how."

Rain stood mutely for a moment. His lips worked, his head shook as if palsied, then he raised the rifle and aimed it at his chest. "So you die."

"No," said Old Alice. "Don't waste your ammo. I'll do it."

And before either of them could stop her, she climbed into the pilot's seat and began her flight check. Annabelle shrugged and climbed after her. Rain Manto couldn't decide if it was a trick or not, finally decided not, and pushed Lincoln in ahead of him. Once they were strapped in, he frisked the two women for weapons, then turned to Lincoln.

Alice groaned when he found the knife.

Annabelle swore when he found the cosh.

Lincoln smiled when he found the bottle in his shirt pocket. "It's a high-protein energy thing," he said. "I use it when I need to stay awake."

"Uppers?"

"You could say that."

Manto decided he needed the stimulant more than the tailor, and emptied the vial. Then he burped. Then his face turned a faint shade of green.

"Damn," he said, and with a menacing jab of his rifle, he staggered out onto the wing and leaned over.

"Alice," said Lincoln, "get us out of here. Now!"

Though Annabelle said something about the rifle, Alice didn't ask questions. She lurched the plane into motion, throwing Rain onto his knees. She spun the plane around and started to taxi. Manto dropped the rifle, but managed to hang on, crawling while shouting incoherently toward the door at Annabelle's right hand. Quickly, she grabbed on to the handle, but Rain had pulled himself up and was staring in at her, froth at his lips, rage in his dead black eyes.

"Climb," Lincoln said.

Alice did, and Rain fell off.

A second later an explosion rocked the cabin, and Lincoln looked to port to see a dark cloud lifting into the dark, starry sky.

"Palmer," he said, "is going to have to be more careful."

"Solitude," breathed Macon Crowley on Farren Upshire's porch, "is one of the great qualities of life."

Old Alice sat beside him on the swing, Palmer was dozing in the rocking chair, and Lincoln was sitting on the steps, watching the three Arabians prancing about in the paddock. He hadn't had much sleep since he'd returned, what with explaining everything to Farren, mollifying Loraleen when Annabelle came with him, and trying to avoid Carmel, who had left several nasty notes under the tailor shop door.

It was worth it, however.

In a way.

The screen door opened, and he looked over his shoulder.

Annabelle and Loraleen were escorting their uncle out to the porch. There were no canes. It was evident the man had dropped at least fifty pounds and was in the process of dropping a good hundred more. Worry, he had said when Lincoln demanded to know how he'd done it; pure and simple worry about his family had done the trick.

"So you didn't need the tail," Lincoln had said, his voice low and toneless.

"Not in the flesh, as it were, no," Farren had laughed. "But its presence lingers on." And he snapped his waistband to show him all that room.

Now the three were smiling, and he guessed it was worth it. The tail and its gold and rubies was gone, but then so were most of the Mantos. The qualifying "most" he reserved for Tremain—that amulet had been around too long to be done in by a bonfire in a cellar— he only hoped that it couldn't work on Manto's ashes.

He sighed, then, and patted the suitcase at his feet.

"When are you leaving for Maine?" Loraleen asked him shyly.

"Now," he said, rose, and bowed to them all. "Right now."

"Alone?" the Bannon sisters asked simultaneously.

"Damn right," Alice told them, and reached for her grapes.

"How you going, son?" Farren said, shaking his hand, the gratitude in his eyes payment enough.

"Dick Pell's going to drive me to the airport in his private bus. Then I'm—"

"Blackthorne!"

Macon Crowley rose, took Alice's hand, and led her into the house. Upshire and the Bannons swung their heads to the right.

"Goddamn you, Lincoln Bartholomew Blackthorne, I had to clean that damned store all by myself!"

Lincoln smiled painfully, grabbed his satchel, and began to run. There was no sense heading for the car on the road; Carmel would be there, enraged and hunting for tailor, if not bear.

Instead, he raced directly for the paddock where the grey mare was waiting. It wouldn't be the most comfortable way to get to New England, but it was better than losing his scalp to a Spaniard.

Besides, he thought as he vaulted the fence, it's the vacation that counts, not the way you get there.